THE REAL WORLD

Christopher Knowlton

THE REAL WORLD

NEW YORK 1984 *Atheneum*

Library of Congress Cataloging in Publication Data

Knowlton, Christopher.
    The real world.

    I. Title.
PS3561.N683B5   1984   813'.54   83-45505
ISBN 0-689-11439-7

FOR MY BROTHERS,

Win and Oliver

"Very well, Thrasymachus," said I. "So you think I am quibbling?"

"I am sure you are."

The Republic of Plato

THE REAL WORLD

1.

Professionals

CALEB SPARROW lied to his father: he had for years. He had lied about his academic performance in college; he had lied about the level of responsibility he held in his summer jobs; and now he lied about how well he was doing at Hooker & Lyman, Inc. He had been at H&L seven months, and to assure his father during lunch at the University Club—they were celebrating Caleb's twenty-fourth birthday—that he was comfortable at the firm, that the work was going well, was grossly misleading. The work was not going well, and to learn the truth Bob Sparrow had only to call John Beauregard, a partner in the firm, Caleb's boss, and by no accident one of Bob Sparrow's fraternity brothers.

He lied to keep their dialogue open. Not that these fibs

fooled his father—they certainly didn't alter Caleb's standing in his father's esteem, where he continued to occupy a middle rung. Unlike his brother, Robert, four years his senior, whose flirtation with socialism, participation in the sixties youth movement, and eventual Christian rebirth severely strained the familial ties, Caleb had done nothing noteworthy to disappoint his parents. He had never been expelled from prep school, arrested for drunken driving, or caught experimenting with hallucinogens. Unfortunately, he, like Robert, had little interest in playing sports, a fact inexplicable to their father, who had been an All-Ivy golfer at Brown and remained an avid, if undistinguished, squash-player. Their apathy meant the family missed the father-son golf and tennis tournaments which made up summer weekends at the Westchester Country Club. It meant Bob Sparrow never had a Little League team to root for or a son to putt with. But it also meant Caleb had his weekends free to bird-watch, a hobby his father assumed he would outgrow the way mothers assumed their daughters would outgrow horses.

These days when Caleb and his father spent an evening together they went to the movies. His father loved Stephen King thrillers and always saw the film versions. Sitting shoulder to shoulder before the lights dimmed, they strove to project a spirit of camaraderie. Caleb nodded at whatever his father said and smiled mindlessly at the blank screen. If they dined together afterward, the discussion revolved around the movie, Robert's latest transgression, or Caleb's finances.

Bob Sparrow belonged to the troop of post-war professionals who entered the ranks of business management at a time when young executives were scarce and the opportunities at the outset of those boom years limitless. The company he had joined as a salesman in 1950, Olympus Brands, now belonged to the Fortune 500, and Sparrow was its President and Chief Executive Officer. Strangers on the avenues recognized him from his photo in *Business Week*; restaurant proprietors knew his name and awarded him choice tables; on weekends he flew his foursome by company helicopter to his favorite golf course and landed on the first tee. Ten years had passed since the divorce, when he had swapped suburbia for city life, and nine since he had married Gretchen Knoedler, an aristocratic Swiss German.

They formed an impressive partnership. She belonged to the Colony Club; he belonged to the University Club, Confederate Club, and, although he didn't own a boat, had recently joined the New York Yacht Club. In a given week they might attend a performance at Lincoln Center, a fund-raising dinner, and a Broadway opening. These gala events were mixed with business gatherings, initiation dinners, and the like, where Bob Sparrow was expected to appear for at least the duration of a cocktail to voice his support for a new educational or arts program, political candidate, or office building.

The Sparrows' relationship had the symmetry of an alliance wrought out of contracts and law. Duties and responsibilities had been divvied up and delegated down through personal secretaries, maids, and chauffeurs. As Robert put it, Bob and Gretchen Sparrow were well coordinated.

At six-two Bob Sparrow possessed the height commonly

cited as an asset in the quest for a corporate presidency. His face was by turns, depending on the season, gunpowder gray, rawhide, belt-leather brown, or that intermediate condition exhibited after a weekend of golf or a convention in Florida, sun-slapped rouge. A fine square head of silver hair, mournful eyes, a mouth with downturned corners, and a sturdy chin—these never changed. It was the face at first glance of a man sad and longsuffering, a face therefore misleading, because his father was not unhappy but rather, in Caleb's opinion, overworked, worn out.

They were seated at a table near the window. The waiter took their order.

"I was at a loss what to give you."

"I would have taken a check, Dad."

"You'd spend it on some broad and have nothing to remember the day by."

"I wish. The business about the broad, I mean."

"I don't follow."

"I wish I had a broad to spend it on."

"None at all?"

"There's a woman in the office. She went to Harvard Business School. But I don't think she's interested."

Bob Sparrow did not pursue the subject.

"I think you're bigger than I am in the chest, so I bought a forty-two."

Caleb stretched the gold ribbon and freed it from a corner of the blue Brooks Brothers box. Inside, under tissue, lay a raincoat, the lining a woefully familiar camel-and-black tartan.

"I wear a forty long, Dad."

"Then we're the same size."

Caleb didn't feel the same size; he felt considerably smaller.

"You shouldn't have any trouble exchanging it. Cost two hundred dollars." Bob Sparrow believed price fairly reflected worth and took every opportunity to remind Caleb what things cost.

"It's a very good coat. I can use it."

"You don't already have one, I hope."

"No." What was one more lie? thought Caleb.

"Next time it will be a check. As a matter of fact, I sent your brother a check for his birthday, but only because Gretchen and I couldn't think of a thing to get him since he claims to have renounced all worldly possessions. Do you know what I got in reply? A note threatening to sue me *and* Olympus Brands if we don't discontinue Chug-A-Lug, that new jerry-jug wine of ours. He insists it's carcinogenic. There was also something about the sinfulness of alcohol, which I guess means he doesn't drink any more."

"He wants to sue you?"

"A holy crusade of some sort. We don't take it too seriously. I'll admit it could be a little embarrassing—his being the son of the President—but I suppose that's his intention."

"I can't believe he wants to sue you." They were interrupted as the appetizers arrived.

Bob Sparrow was delighted with the food and the service. He sampled Caleb's dishes and joked with the waiter about the poor man's paunch and took so much enjoyment in the meal that Caleb began to feel as though

7

it were his father's birthday they were celebrating and not his own. Halfway through his chocolate mousse Bob Sparrow turned introspective.

"Wages, payments for goods and services, taxes and contributions, all stemming from profits, are what make the economy work. I see where I fit into the system and that's a source of comfort. But you know, sometimes you lose track of what's important in life, why you entered business in the first place, and what you hoped to accomplish . . ."

Bob Sparrow stared at his mousse. It was a self-consciously shared moment, and it made Caleb uncomfortable. Why was it, no disrespect intended, that he preferred to hear the generalities of life from almost anyone but his father?

". . . and you make the kind of mistakes and compromises you can't forget."

That part surprised Caleb.

Bob Sparrow, aggressive, driven, was a leader. Caleb could remember the yearbook picture of his father—captain of his college golf team, the slim, crew-cut, jaunty-looking ectomorph with elastic arms, leaning on his driver with a confident, noble air. He could not imagine his father making unforgettable mistakes, not someone who, it seemed, had been born knowing and talking business, which was like growing up comfortable around girls. Caleb, who had begun to feel that joining H&L was *his* first mistake, read the *Wall Street Journal*, *Business Week*, and *Fortune*, but felt like an American in Paris taking his first stab at French. The business terminology, words such as escrow, depreciation, amortization, fiduciaries, still sounded unnatural in his vocabulary. After all those years of schooling, he was a freshman again.

"But I don't think your generation will repeat our mistakes. Growing up with Viet Nam and Watergate, you're bound to be more sophisticated than we ever were. I may worry about Robert, but I have confidence, Caleb, that you personally will make it."

Caleb wished his father wouldn't make the comparison. It wasn't fair to Robert, and it saddled Caleb with a nagging pressure of filial obligation. He wished he could refuse these votes of confidence even if he had to admit that his father meant well.

On the way back to his office, in the lunch-hour crowd bunched up and surging down Fifth Avenue, Caleb thought about "making it." After less than a year in New York City, Caleb knew that what he was expected to make was money. As much as possible—more than he could imagine. That seemed to explain why he and everyone else were there, and he saw no reason to be ashamed of it.

2.

Augean Stables

SPREAD sheets and Dun & Bradstreet reports, proxy statements and glossy annuals were stacked in loose, uneven piles on the floor of Caleb's cubicle in the New York offices of Hooker & Lyman. He had papered the surrounding walls with reams of green computer print-out, the financial data on twelve aerospace companies regurgitated by Compustat. He sat with his fingers pressed to his cheeks, his lower lip protruding, staring down at the digital display of his HP 38E programmable calculator, which displayed a sequence of nines, its response to a problem incorrectly posed or insoluble. Open beside him lay the user's manual, a small, spiral-bound notebook. It offered no advice on how to proceed.

The time was 9 p.m. on the night of his birthday, a

Monday in early June. Until this moment that wedge of black plastic with rows of buttons the size of tacks, lettered and numbered according to their particular arithmetic deed, had solved equations with a finality and certainty he adored. In return he had treated it like a prized possession, carrying it home at night in his briefcase whether or not he had work to do. Now he felt betrayed.

He shut the calculator off, straightened it on his desk, and blew a speck of dust off its face in a gesture of forgiveness before rising from his swivel chair, arching his back, and stretching. Stiff, thirsty, he left his alcove and walked through the soundproofed, fluorescent-lit halls of the firm.

Little of the studying Caleb had done in college—certainly none of the great books he had read—had prepared him for the corporate world. The works of Homer and Thucydides, of Plato and Aristotle, had no direct bearing on a job in business. He had enlisted in a world of facts and figures.

As a research analyst he was required to collect data about a given industry and perform rudimentary financial analysis: calculating growth rates, debt-and-liquidity ratios. Number crunching. The work provided sound preparation for jobs on the financial side of business, which Caleb had been assured was a growth area. He knew there were hundreds who had gone before him working on the same companies—he found their penciled calculations in the margins of the older annuals. The companies had been smaller then, and the researchers had used slide rulers instead of calculators, but otherwise he supposed that the work was the same. He wondered if they had daydreamed, as he did, of the time when they would have their own secretary, apartment, English antiques, and, perhaps, a wife.

The only events which broke up his day were excursions to the coffee machine and the men's room. At the coffee machine in the employees' lounge the ceremony of preparing a cup of coffee gave him a chance to relax, to talk to the secretaries about the Bruce Springsteen concert over the weekend, the status of a husband's job search, the backload in Report Production, or one of their favorite topics, the incompetence of temporaries. Caleb would twist a cup off the Styrofoam stack, splash milk in, add a packet of Sweet 'N Low, and then pour the coffee. This procedure, which he performed efficiently and without variation, nevertheless pleased him simply because it was manual. He took his time, fastened the plastic cap, and clenched a red stir straw in his teeth for the walk back to his desk.

When he had finished his coffee he would visit the men's room and use the urinal and soap and wash his hands. A double set of doors led into the yellow-tiled bathroom; both made vacuum thumps when they closed, one after the other. The researchers' room was just down the hall, and the noise from those doors had bothered Caleb so much during his first month at H&L that he complained to Maintenance. When nothing was done, he spent a lunch hour visiting hardware stores and bought a variety of doorstops which later that night, after everyone had left, he attempted—without success—to affix to the frames.

The trip to the john formally concluded his coffee

break. Caleb went directly to work, careful not to waste the charge of caffeine. He considered himself conscientious.

During his first month on the job, he had trod the same strip of carpet from his desk to Jim Pike's to Report Production and back, over and over. The only sunshine Caleb saw was what fell through the window as he stood in Pike's doorway and reported on his progress. He was surprised how bright and clean that sunshine looked on the carpet: a spill of pale yellow paint. Each day at noon he ordered lunch by phone, had it delivered, and ate in his cubicle. In the tiny, green print-out-papered space he could eat, nap, or doodle out of sight of the rest of the firm. That seeming bit of privacy was a vital aspect of the researchers' working lives; it allowed them to pamper and indulge themselves without each other's knowledge. In actuality nothing remained a secret for long. Caleb knew Grayson Ault kept a can of Bosco in his file cabinet and twice a day heard him mix a cup, using milk from the coffee counter. And Grayson knew Caleb saved paper clips and prided himself on his well-manicured nails.

Caleb's desk had been occupied by a researcher named Penny Singleton who had been fired shortly before he joined the firm. In the drawers he found worry beads, macramé, a squirt gun, an empty lipstick-dispenser, a dozen movie stubs, and four "While You Were Out" slips dated October 6 and inscribed, "Call your mother." Penny, he had heard, saw a movie a day, generally during her extended lunch breaks. She made errors in her arithmetic and, according to Grayson, was persuaded that she would be more comfortable in another profession. Which profession, the firm didn't specify.

Now that the desk was Caleb's he could share the ambitions and frustrations of those who spoke of "the office." The fact that his desk was in a management consulting firm in the Reeves Building on Park Avenue sharply defined who he was. His name was associated with the firm's and he became readily identifiable to people he met through work or socially. Like the birds he had admired in his youth, he could be categorized by order, family, genus, and species.

A hundred and fifty professionals and two hundred general office staff worked in the New York offices which made H&L one of the larger management consulting firms. It was also one of the oldest. After seven months Caleb knew roughly a third of the personnel by name.

At night he walked the halls of H&L without worrying about colliding with secretaries at intersections. Most of the office doors were closed. He heard the whir of the central air-conditioning and the hum of the Xerox machines. If Report Production worked overtime to meet a deadline and ran the press, a low, rolling throbbing could be felt more than heard. One had the sense of the firm as a huge metallic organism pumping money through its arteries.

He slipped change into the Coke machine. The first coin registered with a dry, electric click, but the successive coins fell into a void. A tattoo on the face of the machine failed to produce the can; he rocked the box, spoke to it, stuffed another quarter in the slot before marching out into the hall, disgusted.

A flight of carpeted stairs separated the twenty-fifth floor from the twenty-sixth floor. The Managing Partner had installed the staircase to save members of the firm the trouble of riding the elevators between floors. Although this was termed an efficiency move, Caleb suspected it had to do with Langely Insurance, the firm which occupied the floors above H&L and packed the elevator between 9 a.m. and 4 p.m. with salesmen in ill-fitting suits and thick Countess Mara ties, toupeed portfolio managers, an assortment of clerks, secretaries, and delivery boys who laughed and spoke freely about their personal lives. Their H&L counterparts, more soberly attired, rode the elevator in silence; nevertheless, the Managing Partner wanted to minimize the mingling of Langely employees and members of H&L's professional staff.

Caleb took the stairs two at a time and checked the fit of his necktie knot as he crossed the hall. The security guard slept at the reception desk, his head in his arms. For a moment, passing the Chairman's office, Caleb felt like opening the door and peeking in, just to get an idea from the decor how the boss lived. Caleb had not met the Chairman—as far as he knew, no researcher had—and since so many of the firm's officers looked alike, he would not have recognized him if he passed him in the hall.

Report Production was housed in three rooms: Copy Processing, which resembled the newsroom of a small newspaper, with five micom terminals and a glassed-in room for proofreading; Graphics, where charts and exhibits for the reports were laid out; and Printing, which contained two IBM Series 3, Model 60 copiers, the press, and gadgets for laminating and attaching spiral bindings. Every client assignment required at least one bound report, anywhere from fifteen to a hundred pages long, containing information about the study approach, the findings, and the recommendations, and printed according to the firm's strict format, requiring study assertions, major and minor headline sentences, subheadings and supporting assertions and concluding with appendices. In most cases this report was also converted into slides or transparencies for a visual presentation. Generally, a researcher oversaw the production of the report, a process referred to as "shepherding" which required periodically "goosing" the supervisor to ensure deadlines were met, and inevitably meant proofing the work of the proofreaders.

That afternoon Caleb had deposited his project team's report-in-progress on the desk of the Director of Report Production—to be typed "rush"—but had neglected to check back with her at five to be certain a micom operator would be on hand during the night shift until the job was finished. No lights were on in RP. The document, entitled *An Executive Compensation Strategy for Benefact Corp*, sat untouched in a neat stack on the Director's desk. Caleb flipped through the pages, noticing that his handwriting had grown tight and cramped in the last seven months, the letters mere sticks and slashes. Three exhibits were missing from this preliminary draft—those he had been struggling to finish when his calculator jammed.

Caleb had been mildly surprised, considering the number of hours he had worked, when a raise did not automatically follow the completion of his first assignment. But his job-end appraisal stated explicitly that better data interpretation and more initiative were expected of him. Competence they took for granted. He was required to excel. To demonstrate his initiative he had assumed responsibility for more aspects of this project than he could keep track of. Now, after nine weeks of labor, with the data gathered and the analysis nearly complete, the numbers had begun to look wrong, and, fatigued, he was making foolish mistakes. He would have enough trouble just meeting the deadline, let alone excelling.

Tramping down the carpeted stairs to the twenty-fifth floor, lazy about lifting his feet, he slipped near the bottom and fell hard on his rear end. He slid out onto the floor and lay there staring up at the soundproofing, his back on the bottom steps. Down the hall came Omar Sahib, a debonair Indian educated at the London School of Economics, the former captain of the firm's squash team who had recently been made a partner in the Technology Management Group. Without looking down at Caleb, he stepped over his legs and started up the stairs. Standard H&L operating procedure, thought Caleb: walk in single file, keep moving, no talking in the halls. Anger welled up; he hurt. Some birthday this had turned into.

He had hoped to take Diane Landry out for a drink. She was a consultant, which placed her above the researchers but below the principals and partners in the firm's hierarchy. She had joined the firm a year ago, straight out of business school. Caleb had first met her when, at Pike's suggestion, he sought her advice on beverage bottling, an industry she had researched for a professor at Harvard.

"Beverage bottling is a bore. The truth is I only did the work because the professor wrote great recommendations."

She was a strawberry blonde with lively blue eyes; her quick looks skipped back and forth from his face to the work on her desk and softened to an amused caress whenever he intercepted them. She was the most forthright person he had met at H&L, and for the next ten minutes she showered him with information, observations, and opinions about which company led the industry, which lacked management expertise, which had connections with organized crime. He liked her immediately and to keep her talking he confided his ambition to attend business school.

"They should make it a one-year program. The second year is a waste of time. About all you do is interview. But if you like Monopoly you'll like business school, because that's all it is—games. Of course, there *are* trade-offs. You sacrifice two years of income. Plus the pressure does funny things to you. I gained almost fifteen pounds. I've been dieting ever since."

"*You* have to diet!" He had been struck by her spidery arms and the sharp corners her shoulders made under her blouse.

"Was that intended as a compliment?"

"I see what you mean. It's just that you look perfectly . . . perfectly nice." He meant skinny.

She smiled at him, which set the hammock of his heart in motion. "So do you."

The night of his birthday seemed a logical night to invite her out, and yet he had postponed asking her until late in the afternoon, walking into her office without knocking and stiffly making the invitation as though it were a professional obligation. But if his manner offended her, she didn't show it; swiveling in her chair to face him, she held up the list of survey calls she had to make to California. These were to be followed by a team dinner at the Palm.

"Then I have to read up on pharmaceuticals, so I can brief the team tomorrow. I can do that at home in the bath. I know more about them now than I did in my hippy stage."

"Baths?"

"Drugs. As a hippy I *never* bathed."

She was legitimately busy, so Caleb was not disappointed when she said no: he was relieved. She was two years older, reputedly a bit cuckoo—she had gone to Bennington, a consultant had told him with a smirk—and was good-looking enough to have her choice of the men of the firm. Bad odds. On top of that, he had yet to make up his mind what his own objectives were and to what extent they were honorable. Then again, honorable or not, soaping her back while she sat in the bath had to be a splendid way to spend an evening. Instead, he was sitting on the floor of the reception area of Hooker & Lyman, rubbing his butt.

He stood up too quickly and was dizzy. Walking as though balancing a book on his head, he navigated the halls, left and left again, toward his desk, where the Bufferin bottle lay beside the stapler in the bottom right drawer; he prayed it was not empty. The cap came off with a pop and the last tablets spilled out onto his palm. He chewed four at once, then worked his tongue over his molars to dislodge the bitter crumbs. He swallowed them dry, staring into a photograph of the client tacked over his desk.

The client was Jack Ransome, President and Chief Executive Officer of Benefact Corp, the third-largest manufacturer of jet engines and the eleventh company on the Fortune 500. Ransome was widely publicized for his outspokenness on issues ranging from regulation, which he abhorred, to the Republican Party, which he supported, and for his flamboyant administrative style, which the *Wall Street Journal* found "nothing if not bold and imaginative." In the three years since he was hired away from a rival aerospace company, he had generated considerable controversy by firing most of the twenty divisional vice-presidents and rerouting the company's strategic direction. Benefact Corp had retained H&L to review the compensation package for the top management group, with special attention to Ransome's salary.

Caleb had cut the photo from the most recent annual report, where it appeared on the first page along with the President's letter, a high-spirited description of the year's events in which Ransome expressed satisfaction with the results and his affection and esteem for his colleagues, from his Chief Operating Officer to the lowest errand boy, "without whom there would be no Benefact Corporation." In the photograph Ransome, a tall, thick-trunked man in his mid-fifties, stood behind a desk many times the size of Caleb's, his arms straight and spread as though he were holding down the desk and the floor and the corporation. Caleb had read in a magazine article that Ransome packed a Colt .45 in a vest holster, for self-defense, and recommended that other CEOs do the same. He enjoyed fishing, horseback riding, but, above all, managing. His foremost pleasure in life was the orchestration and motivation of human resources. He was said to dread retirement.

Early in the assignment Caleb and Jim Pike, the thirty-two-year-old principal on the team, had combined an interview with Ransome and a visit to the highly successful Hegel Industries Division of Benefact Corp. They took a train from Grand Central to Bridgeport, where a limousine met them at the station and drove them into the suburban Connecticut countryside. An asphalt driveway curled through acres of freshly mowed lawn, past a man-made pond in the shape of an H. The office building, a castle of glass, did not reflect the cloudless sapphire sky, the vibrant green grass, or the white swans paddling back and forth in the pond. The glass encased the building like polished black armor.

"Bulletproof, I bet," said Caleb. "I was expecting Quonset huts and hangars."

"It's nothing compared to Moore Corporation out in San Diego," said Pike. "Rick Moore graduated from USC and was a center for the Trojans. For corporate headquarters he had his architects design a twenty-story mausoleum in the shape of a Trojan helmet. You ever get out there, take a look at it."

Pike had brought Caleb along to take notes in the meeting; Pike was to do the talking.

On the second floor they were met by Peggy, a plump secretary whose mauve eye make-up could not conceal her melancholy. As she led them down a narrow corridor to the room she referred to as Mr. Ransome's country office, she asked if they were from Manhattan and expressed her regret that she didn't live there. She held the office door open for them.

Ransome had the solid build of a linebacker. Dressed in a navy blue suit, a starched, vanilla shirt, and a green-striped silk necktie, he stood at ease in the center of the room. He greeted them without smiling, impassive, then showed them to a couch and urged them to be seated. Pillowy, the couch seemed to suck Caleb down and hold him. An attractive brunette woman in a tennis dress stared adoringly at them from a snapshot on Ransome's desk.

"I might as well let you know at the outset that I have never approved of consultants." The admission was delivered in a flat voice without apology. "Never saw the need for them."

"It's a matter of how you perceive the function," said Pike politely. "We are generalists. Most of our team has manufacturing experience, and I have worked in the aircraft industry; however, we don't know your company, and we won't tell you your job."

Ransome responded with a bassoon laugh.

"What we will do," Pike continued, "is study, watch, and listen in an effort to get a sense of the nature of the management task, which is a key variable in any compensation assignment. We want to be sure that what we see in the field jibes with our analysis. Please view us as a resource. We're at your disposal."

"Don't worry, Mr. Pike. I always get my money's worth."

Peggy entered, bent over a tray of cups and saucers. Ransome was served first; he crossed his legs, which brought one shoe on a level with Caleb's head. He sipped his coffee, swallowed; his Adam's apple went down like a yo-yo.

"Let's begin," he said. "The first thing you should know is that I am *the* man for this job. To be blunt, I have a big mind. My line managers have little minds. As you might expect, this does not make me popular. But, frankly, corporate management is no popularity contest."

He replaced the cup in the saucer. "I believe, above all, in strength. I don't pretend to be a practicing Christian any more. It's an allegiance, like belonging to a club, but mostly I find it meaningless. I believe that if no God exists, and there is no reason to believe one does, then there is only man, and man must be as noble and strong and perfect as he can be. This is not popular thinking in our egalitarian age. The average man will resent this kind of thinking because he hasn't the will or ability to perfect himself."

Caleb took notes: minds pretend Christian, club no God.

"Look what this equality nonsense has given us—a second-rate world, a world of mediocrity. Nothing is beautiful, nothing is well made; nothing lasts. This country lacks strength, intensity, creativity, and discipline, and I don't think we can afford to behave this way much longer. It's decadent and inflationary. It's feminine.

"What is my remedy?" He was looking out the window now and seemed to have forgotten them for the moment. Perhaps he saw himself addressing a convention audience or the Business Roundtable. "We need energy, enthusiasm, imagination. We need personality!" He took a breath, looked at and past Caleb, who, in turn, looked questioningly at Pike.

"Now, I've got hundreds of branch managers, but they dress, act, talk so much alike that I can hardly keep their names straight. Forget it when it comes to their wives. And those are people, not robots. I don't think they want to be thought of as people, though. I think it makes them uncomfortable. How can I have confidence in them?" He drained the cup.

"I will risk being called an elitist. It doesn't bother me

because I have truth on my side. All men are not created equal. Some are better than others. That is fact. That is truth. And those who are better must lead. We need *leadership*. If you've got a little free time on this project, why don't you see if you can come up with a formula for that?"

Ransome bored in his ear with his pinky. Caleb, watching, no longer taking notes, was mystified by Ransome's corporate evangelism.

The big man swung himself agilely out of his chair, which gave Caleb a glimpse of the gun in its holster, and crossed to the window. "We placed the swans in the pond this morning. We spend twenty grand a year on those birds for feed, veterinary bills, and transportation to and from Florida. They're worth it—magnificent creatures! I would be quite content if, in a reincarnation, I was a corporate swan."

Half an hour later Caleb rolled onto his side to fight his way out of the couch. As he shook Ransome's hand—the fingers as thick and hard as rolls of quarters—Caleb couldn't resist a personal question. "Did you ever play football?" he asked.

"I was a shot-putter."

Pike and Caleb's guide through the Hegel Industries plant was a shrill little man, unabashedly enthusiastic, who apologized for the fact that the low, hangar-like structure wasn't as large as the Boeing plant. That plant was so vast it had its own weather, if they could imagine it. This building was roughly the size of two football fields placed end to end. He led them along an assembly line, boasting that Hegel Industries jet engines were the most advanced and maintenance-free jet engines in the world, and had been since the Second World War.

From a Plexiglas observation booth in the test center they watched a group of white-smocked engineers roll out a circus cannon, the sort used by Ringling Brothers, Barnum & Bailey for firing the human cannonball. They positioned it twenty yards from a mounted Penguin 10 turbo fan jet, a silver canister the size of a small car.

"That cannon is loaded with thirty pounds of gravel. They're going to fire it into that prototype of the P-10 with the engine running as a test for durability. These test engineers are the hot-rodders of the industry. When the test is over, they'll mount that engine on a 727 outside and take it up for a spin, see how she rides."

The concrete floor under Caleb's feet rumbled as the engine smoked and shivered on its mount. The engineers secured their earmuffs and stepped back. One lit the cannon's fuse and both dropped to the ground. A thunderous explosion shook the Plexiglas window; gray flannel smoke obscured the engine from view. There followed a huge cacophonous choking, then the engine caught its breath and resumed roaring. The engineers rose and shook hands and waved at the observation booth. The guide gave them fingers-to-palm applause.

"They do the same thing using chickens to simulate flying into flocks of birds. Eastern has placed an advance order for a hundred of these engines to be delivered in a year's time. That's confidential, of course."

On the test track an engineer stood beside a pile of

25

baseball-sized rocks and tossed them, bemusedly, into the engine's mouth. The P-10 gnashed on them, gulped, and spat them out its tail.

The guide briefed them on the safety features of the Hegel engines; he brought their attention to a framed black-and-white photograph of a Penguin 10. "This one took two hundred pounds of gravel, forty chickens, a stepladder, and one test engineer—poor bastard—who stepped too close. It still got off the ground."

That was Caleb's only trip to a Benefact Corp division. Pike went back to interview other officers and inspect other plants, but by then the data had begun to pile up, and the consensus was that Caleb's time was best spent on the arduous task of organizing and analyzing it. He had been at his desk all day, every day, ever since.

3.

A Westchester Lad

C A L E B kept the photo of Ransome tacked to the cubicle wall to serve as his conscience during moments of lackadaisy. Over his desk Grayson had a quote by Horst Mahler, a West German revolutionary, taken from his 1973 trial: "You don't talk to the stooges of capitalism. You shoot them." According to Grayson, Mahler today had a successful career as a consultant offering businessmen workshops and seminars on Marxism.

Tonight, facing the photo, Caleb was depressed by the career gulf that separated him from Ransome, and he wondered where Ransome would place him in his great corporate chain of being.

Caleb had been born in the Northern Westchester Hospital Center, June 7, 1960. The Sparrows then lived

in Katonah, a countrified town at the north end of the
Saw Mill River Parkway boasting its own Pappagallo. The
house—four bedrooms, three baths, a living room (out of
bounds for the boys), dining room, family room, and
two-car garage—was in the Cow Lane development, where
the Block Association had paid to have the pavement removed. His father commuted; his mother, Jane, belonged
to the more verdant of the two garden clubs. Both he and
his brother attended the local private day school. Caleb
spent his free time birding and wishing Louisa Fisher, who
lived up the street and who received in the mail an anony-
mous ID bracelet, would requite his love. Both boys fell
back a year in schooling as they accompanied their mother,
after the divorce, on her northward migration through
Connecticut, Rhode Island, Massachusetts, and, eventually,
New Hampshire, into the arms of Rupert Shaw, the
headmaster of Mannes Academy, a small militaristic prep
school which rejected Caleb on the basis of his inability
to spell "separate" and "anglophile." He prepped instead at
Salisbury School in the Berkshires. He had a pleasant, if
uneventful, four years there earning his highest grades in
Latin, and was accepted at Brown, because he was the son
of a prominent alumnus, and at Denison in Ohio. To Bob
Sparrow's chagrin he chose Denison which he preferred
for its size and rural setting.

In college Caleb majored in Ancient Civilization and
kept up with his course work. His longest paper, written
hastily, was on the fall of the Roman Empire, and in his
professor's opinion it relied too heavily (fifty-two foot-
notes) on Gibbon. He wrote letters to the campus newspaper protesting the reinstatement of draft registration and

shortened hours at the student pub; he dated, slept late, and had his first serious romance. During his senior year he began his career deliberations in earnest.

He chose a career in business by default.

His work experience had been limited to summer jobs: paving driveways in Westchester; scooping ice cream and waiting tables for the minimum wage on Martha's Vineyard; and working for a New York publishing house in a clerical job which required him to process warehouse orders for books. And his academic credentials and his extracurricular accomplishments were not strong, which discouraged him from applying right away to graduate schools or considering a career in academia. Caleb viewed teaching as another form of classroom confinement, and he was sure that beyond the campus walls the true adventures of life were unfolding. As for government and politics, they simply didn't interest him.

His father had some bearing on his choice. For one thing, Bob Sparrow's career was familiar and comprehensible to Caleb—he had grown up with it. And when they discussed career possibilities, Bob Sparrow said there were only two fields a gentleman went into: business or law. "That's what my old man told me," said his father. "I'm passing it on."

Caleb didn't consider himself a gentleman in the strict sense of the word. On the other hand, he couldn't see himself in a hard hat either. He did *look* right for the business world. He was somewhat round-shouldered with slim hips and long legs. The features of his face were to scale but not, in his opinion, remarkable. Despite handsome, deep-set brown eyes, his natural expression was glum, like that of all the men in his family. He had the perfectly ordinary face of a Westchester Wasp.

When Caleb sat down to write his résumé, he listed Economics as his minor. In fact, he had taken just one economics course and financial accounting, for which he had received a B. He wrote the résumé conscious that the Caleb Sparrow who emerged sounded more experienced and better equipped to work in business than the real he. The last section of the résumé, the section devoted to interests, gave Caleb the most trouble. How could he explain to a Director of Personnel that he wasn't an athlete, didn't sail, golf, or play tennis? Tell him the truth—that he enjoyed bird-watching, that he walked for exercise— and he would be labeled peculiar and not invited back. What businessman wanted a naturalist on his staff? Finally, Caleb listed squash and sailing among his interests. Until he took a squash lesson he would plead injury when invited to play. Sailing was strictly a matter of terminology, and he intended to buy a book on the subject.

Caleb did not begin hunting for a job until the fall after he graduated. He had successfully completed his education and, declaring that he was entitled to a break, he went back to Martha's Vineyard, where for the months of July and August he did little more than lie on the beach. A job-hunter's manual said that a suntan made a favorable first impression in an interview. If that was so, then in all probability he would never be forgotten. On the beach he fantasized about working for some successful middle-aged man who would adopt him as a protégé and insist he marry one of his beautiful daughters, raised on caviar and champagne, who lived at home on the family's Long Island estate. When he confessed this months later to his roommate, Dale Abernathy, one night during his introduction to Armagnac, Dale's response—"Admit it, Sparrow. You went into it, like everyone else, to get laid"—missed the point. A job in business offered prestige and security. And he wanted romance, and business looked romantic.

In September Caleb began to interview wherever he had a contact or could persuade someone to see him: at commercial and investment banks, insurance companies, conglomerates, advertising agencies, and diversified communication companies. Most of his interviews stemmed from his father or from friends of his father. He accepted politely what help he could get, aware that his résumé, unescorted, was a faulty apparatus for securing interviews. During his first two, with Morgan Stanley and McKinnsy, out of respect for the interviewers, he had let them do all the talking; during the third, with Shearson/American Express, for fear he would be asked questions he couldn't answer, *he* did all the talking. Eventually he achieved an uneasy balance of questions and answers, committing only occasional gaffes such as losing his place in a passionate explanation of why he wanted to enter commercial banking or calling the interviewer by the wrong name. The one interview which had gone splendidly was followed by a form letter apologizing for the company's inability to hire him and a promise to keep his résumé on file.

To prepare for his first interview at H&L, Caleb had his suit cleaned, trimmed his hair with paper scissors, and clipped his fingernails, giving them a conservative flare by squaring off the fronts. He had practiced smiling at the mirror and rehearsed the scenario in which he explained to a crestfallen interviewer that he had a number of other offers meriting consideration, most of them generous, and that he would try to reach a decision in the coming week.

The receptionist at H&L wrote down his name and asked him to take a seat. The reception area, a low-ceilinged room with thick wall-to-wall carpeting, potted plants, and modern furniture, reminded Caleb of living rooms in Katonah. He spread his arm over the back of his chair to effect a casual look. He crossed his legs, left ankle over right thigh. A young red-haired man about his age entered through a varnished wood door, head lowered, chin doubled. Only inches separated his freckled face from the oversized sheets of paper which he was rustling and shaking into an even stack. When he reached the door beside the couch, a hand emerged, groped for the knob, and clutched it. He lost control of the papers, and the top of the stack slid out and cascaded to the floor. Caleb jumped up to help him. The young man knelt, losing more of the pile in the process.

"I'll get them," said Caleb. "You hold the pile."

"Here for an interview?" asked the young man, using his chin to hold the papers in place.

Caleb nodded.

"Know your three greatest strengths and weaknesses. They always ask that. But go easy on the weaknesses." Caleb thanked him for the advice. "And try to relax," the young man called back.

Easy for you to say, thought Caleb.

A telephone rang and the receptionist answered it in a whisper. "No," she said, "no . . . nope."

The next man to enter was Tony Graves, the Director of Personnel.

The rule of thumb when hunting for an entry-level job in New York, Caleb had been advised, was to avoid the Personnel Departments. These personnel executives were experts in what had come to be called human-resource management, but actually had limited authority and played only a minor role in a company's hiring practices. According to Bob Sparrow, they were frequently passed over by headhunters working directly with the boards and by officers doing their own hiring. Caleb had been referred to Tony Graves and believed it would be a dead end.

Graves was dressed meticulously, in a narrow-lapelled, gray, chalk-striped suit; his gold tie clasp matched his initialed cufflinks. And he wore a tanning-gel. A thin brown film, drying on the edges, was spread over his cheeks and under his eyes. He was in a hurry and had no sooner shaken Caleb's hand than he turned and, ordering Caleb to follow, retreated from the room.

In Graves's office Caleb sat facing an original M.C. Escher print depicting red ants crawling over a Möbius strip. He settled on an approach he hoped reflected his maturity and goal-orientation. He offered a brief synopsis of his recent past, describing his educational background and listing the subjects he had studied in college. Then he took a breath and explained the evolution of his interest in business, how his father was a role model and had introduced him to the challenges and rewards of corporate life. Consulting, he went on, particularly interested him because it provided the opportunity to work in a variety of industries. It offered

33

the broadest management experience and therefore the best initiation into the business world. During Caleb's introduction Graves removed a thread from a trouser leg and disguised a quick pick of his nose as a rub-pinch. When Caleb finished, Graves looked up, curious, as though he'd been waiting for Caleb to stop.

"Is this your first interview?"

"No, sir." He had thought he was off to a good start. There was an outside chance that Graves was attempting to intimidate him; he had an aloofness which Caleb couldn't read. Caleb abandoned his interview plan and gave simple one-sentence answers to the next few questions.

Graves swiveled to face the window, where the upper stories of neighboring buildings jutted into the pewter sky. He put a hand to his chin, rotated his jaw, then ran his fingers down his throat.

"We're interested in a particular kind of young man here at H&L. We want the kind who, at home, makes his bed and cleans up after himself. We want the model student, the class leader, the Eagle Scout. Most of the professionals here have years of experience in the fields they consult in. They have expertise. Our clients don't care who they are or what they look like so long as they've got that expertise. Young men like yourself, right out of college, with only BAs, have Romper Room for experience."

He slapped Caleb's résumé with the back of his hand. "Do you honestly think our clients are interested in your knowledge of ancient history? They just want to know that you're better than the next guy and that you'll bust your butt to keep them happy. We work sixty to eighty hours a week, so this is not an easy business, Caleb."

"I'd be bored in a job that didn't make demands on me."

"I know why consulting has become so popular and it isn't for the love of work—it's (a) for the prestige, and (b) for the money."

Caleb shrugged. "To tell you the truth, I don't know what the compensation is."

"That a fact?"

Reclining in the chair with his legs outstretched, Graves began to read through the résumé. "Let's see what we got here. Squash player. Play on the team at Denison?"

"Recreational."

"We have a good team here at H&L. . . . Have you applied to business schools?"

"No, sir."

"Most of our research analysts are deferred admits. They have an acceptance from a top school and they are here to get two or three years of intensive work experience before attending."

Graves turned the résumé over, saw that nothing was on the back, and began to jot notes on a ruled evaluation form. "I'll tell you honestly, Caleb, that I am not comfortable with your limited quantitative background. We have a strong numbers-orientation in this firm."

"I'm convinced I could do the work." Caleb was prepared to explain how he had benefitted from bird-watching, developing an appetite for knowledge and an attentiveness to detail (traits indispensable to the ornithologist in the field). He would make the case that these skills were transferable to business. Attention to detail didn't sound particularly grand as an attribute, but it helped build an image of reliability.

Graves wrote in silence, then suddenly put down his pen.

"So, how is your father? Did you know that Olympus Brands Company is one of our clients?"

"I didn't. I *do* know that Mr. Beauregard is a friend of my father's. I believe it was he who arranged for this interview."

"We did a strategy assignment for them a year ago in which we recommended they introduce the frozen pizza and that jerry-jug wine which has become so popular. Beauregard headed that study. What kind of year is Olympus having?"

"Record earnings."

"That's something. I guess fast-foods are recession-proof. They say it's a great management team."

"Yes."

Caleb, determined not to let his father and Olympus Brands become the focus of the interview, did not volunteer any more information.

"This has been very informative. There's someone I'd like you to meet—Jim Pike in the Strategy Group. Pike is one of the firm's youngest and most promising principals. I suggested that he take you to lunch. Wait here a minute."

Alone, Caleb chastised himself for letting Graves end the interview before he had fully discussed his abilities. The résumé and evaluation form lay on Graves's desk in an open manila folder. Listening for footsteps, he rose and sneaked a look. Under the word "Appearance" Caleb read:

Gimbel's shirt.
Dad's hand-me-down suit.
Forgot to polish shoes.

This entry was followed by a series of more random entries, some difficult to read:

Doesn't seem hungry for job. No athlete here. Little business savvy. Analytical skills? Could be a sleeper. Compensation—if hired, position at first quartile of salary range.

At the bottom of the page, circled:

Olympus Brands.

Jim Pike gave the lunch plans an added twist by inviting two researchers, Leonard Pridgeon and Grayson Ault. They walked to the Waldorf. In the Peacock Alley Restaurant, Pike sat facing Caleb, his elbows on the pink tablecloth. The movements of his head and hands were quick and assured, and when he spoke to Caleb he leaned toward him and looked him steadily in the eye. He had short, lustrous black hair combed neatly to the side, a face with strong cheek bones, and a slender, curved nose. He recommended the avocado salad as an appetizer; all four ordered it. Leonard and Grayson looked to be about Caleb's age and were dressed in identical blue three-piece suits; both looked sullen in the roll of subordinates. Leonard, the stocky one, only infrequently looked up from his food. Grayson appeared to be counting the number of people dining.

"How many?" said Pike.

"Fifty." Grayson, sandy-haired, had round, cherubic cheeks, and a surprisingly husky voice, as though the one had evolved to offset the other.

"So say one-fifty for lunch at fifteen bucks a shot and three hundred for dinner at forty bucks a shot, maybe three hundred days a year. I'd ballpark the gross at $4,275,000 a year."

"Assuming there's no seasonal trade," said Grayson.

Both men nodded.

Pike broached the subject of Caleb's candidacy. "I take it you're single?"

Caleb had a mouthful of avocado. ". . . Yes."

"We prefer that. Family life is, for the most part, incompatible with this type of work, at least at the researcher level. The deadlines are numerous and the demands on your time constant. And I should add that we don't meet girls through this kind of work. This is not like a bank training program, but then, living in New York, you see girls everywhere. They're hard to avoid. If girls are your recreation, you shouldn't have too much trouble. If they're your vocation, then perhaps you should consider another firm."

He fished his lips and slurped his coffee. "As you may know, H&L is best known for its quantitative orientation. To give people an idea of what we mean by that, Grayson and I always give a little demonstration. Grayson, fire away."

Grayson leaned forward and quizzed Pike in the bark of quarterback calling signals.

"Multiply $3/16$ by $4/9$."

"—$1/12$!"

"Convert $7/13$ to a percentage."

"—53.8!"

"Square root of 18."

"—4.24!"

Pike studied Caleb's reaction while effortlessly calculating the answers, as if he had unhitched his eyes from his mental processes.

"He can do sines and cosines, too," said Grayson.

The entrees arrived.

"If you can add, subtract, multiply, and divide as fast as I can, then you can think on your feet. And that's what you need to be able to do in this business because at presentations clients will ask questions you couldn't possibly anticipate. In most cases I can answer them. I consider myself an expert on four industries: automotive, insurance, telecommunications, and oil and gas exploration and production. I have been offered senior-level positions in all of them. I could accept a job tomorrow and double my salary. But I consider myself an idea man, not a manager. I'll stay with H&L until I get bored with it."

Pike stabbed a scalloped potato with his fork. He smiled conspiratorially at Grayson as he asked the next question. "If you've done your homework, Caleb, you know what we've got to offer you. I'd like to hear what you've got to offer us."

Caleb stared down at an unrecognizable collection of vegetables on his plate. "I suppose, above all, I can offer you my wholehearted commitment. Hard work. A good business sense."

"Will you pardon me if I say that we take that for granted? What else?"

Caleb had the impression they were calibrating his intelligence, indexing and cross-referencing his every gesture and remark. "Maturity."

"What else?"

"Good manners."

"What about friendship?"

"Sure."

"Caleb, if you work for us, you're going to spend a lot of time in our company. You damn well better like us. What I want to know is if you are, professionally speaking, hungry, because you don't look too hungry to me. You look like a well-fed college kid who doesn't know the meaning of overtime. Look at Grayson here. You see what I mean about hungry? Grayson's father is a postal clerk."

"—Postmaster."

"And if his father weren't a postal clerk, do you think he would have been *summa cum laude* at Williams or be working for us today? You've got to have his mixture of pride, insecurity, and impatience. I've got it myself. Makes you hungry."

"I've got it." Pride, anyway, thought Caleb, enough to find this whole interview procedure deeply embarrassing.

"We want you to feel like someone bigger than you is holding your head under water," Pike continued. "Then you are going to get mad, and you are going to fight like hell, and we are going to get a full day's work out of you."

"This mustard has got some jump to it," said Pridgeon, looking up.

The lunch proceeded in painful increments, question by question. Pike allowed him a bite of food every few minutes, but Caleb only nibbled. Pike asked him about his grades, his thesis, his summer jobs, his upbringing, pushing and poking him with questions. By the time the waiter brought the check, Caleb's jacket hung over the back of his chair, perspiration showed under each arm, and he sat, slouched forward, hands in his lap, wishing it were over and asking himself what prevented him from telling them to their faces what he thought of their petty, claustrophobic firm.

A week later a slim ivory envelope arrived bearing the Hooker & Lyman insignia. The letter requested further interviews and specified a time and date for them. He had averaged an interview a day since his first visit to H&L—had even laughed in the one at Young & Rubicam, which had made a good impression. But, it was now late October and studying his situation realistically, he was no further along in his job search than he had been a month before. He allowed that the letter was a good sign, a patch of blue sky, and celebrated with the purchase of two quart bottles of Rolling Rock beer, which he drank feeling woozy and content in front of his father's TV, his feet on the coffee table.

The day came and, as Caleb had expected, Graves delivered him to John Beauregard's office and departed. The partner's face was vaguely familiar, either because Caleb had seen it at one of Bob and Gretchen's dinner parties or because it bore a strong resemblance to Bob Sparrow's face. Beauregard was the same age and had the same short hair and square sideburns; he even wore the identical Saks polka-dot tie Bob Sparrow had worn to Caleb's college graduation. The difference between the two men was a faint but permanent expression of surprise, as though Beauregard had yet to get over his good fortune. He had a wide, loose mouth which produced, on command, a jovial smile.

"You even look like the old man," said Beauregard after they shook hands; Beauregard's felt as smooth and slippery as plastic. "That's fine, just fine. He's some kind of guy. What a golfer."

After urging Caleb to be seated, Beauregard said he had heard positive things about Caleb and could tell from his résumé that he was an enterprising young man. He mentioned that he had two sons, twins, who had applied to Salisbury School and had been turned down. Getting them into prep school had been a problem. He confessed to writing essay questions for them and said he didn't have much confidence in them to get through college, but then that was the luck of the draw. At a loss for anything else to say, he picked up his phone, dialed his secretary, and instructed her to send in Pike.

A moment later the door opened a foot, and Pike stepped in. He nodded to Caleb, and, without a word, his walk trim and cocksure, crossed the room and, turning, hopped up so he sat on the windowsill with his thighs spread flat. He sat still in arm-crossed complacency while Beauregard gave him an expectant, questioning look; then he shrugged, his smile wire-thin. Beauregard spoke slowly. "Caleb, we are impressed with your background and your potential for consulting work."

Pike coughed and Beauregard looked over at him again before continuing. Consulting firms, he explained, generally did not hire BAs, but H&L was prepared to make exceptions when they recognized unusual talent. Few other jobs could offer the same kind of intensive business experience or such broad exposure to business problems.

Conscious that he had not said more than ten words since the interview began, Caleb tried to add to his total. He said he believed what Beauregard said was true.

Pike slipped off the windowsill and walked behind Caleb's chair. Out of the corner of his eye Caleb could see Pike flashing fingers at Beauregard and understood that they had not made up their minds how much to pay him. A long silence followed as Beauregard's lips moved and he counted.

"We are prepared to make you an offer," he said, relaxing. "We will pay you eighteen thousand dollars a year. Now, that may not overwhelm you, but it *is* generous relative to other industries."

Pike recommended that Caleb take a day or two to consider the offer.

Caleb nodded without comprehending. He had an offer; all the talk, the selling was over. He had expected this to be a moment of sheer euphoria, but in fact he felt little more than relief. He was who he had hoped he was after all: someone smart enough to get a job at H&L. He noticed how uncomfortable they looked as they waited for his reply. Were they already having second thoughts about offering him the job, or simply worried he would not accept? His options were to delay acceptance, which meant thanking them and exiting awkwardly to brood over his decision, or to accept the job on the spot, sealing his fate and perhaps impressing them with his enthusiasm, at the moment limited, for working at H&L. Some damning remark by his father about a colleague's inability to make a decision floated into his head and promptly reshaped itself in the form of a dare.

"I don't need to think about it. I'll take it." There, he had said it.

"I told you he'd take it," Pike said to Beauregard. "That's a dinner you owe me."

Welcome, they said. Welcome to H&L, welcome.

4.

The Blackball

A PROFICIENCY at squash seemed a business prerequisite. During his first week on the job Caleb had asked his father for a lesson and Bob Sparrow was delighted to oblige.

They arranged to meet at the Confederate Club, a stone fortress on Park Avenue, devoted, as best Caleb could tell, to preserving the recipe for the mint julep and a man's right to exclusive privacy. Gilt-framed portraits of Robert E. Lee and Stonewall Jackson hung in the marble foyer. Two muskets crossed barrels in a large antique glass display case, along with a first edition of *The Red Badge of Courage* and a lavender garter. Caleb was greeted by a black man in livery who led him up two flights of a wide, semicircular staircase to a booth in the locker room. He presented Caleb with a bulky terrycloth bathrobe—presumably for the trip to and from the showers. Caleb drew the curtain and changed.

Bob Sparrow was whacking forehands up and down the side wall when Caleb entered the court. That day all the lines in his father's face ran vertically: the pair of creases between his eyebrows, the edges of jowl from his cheekbones to the corners of his thin mouth. Caleb tempered the sudden exhilarating thought that he had a chance to win—there was a twenty-eight-year difference in their ages—with the more honorable sentiment that he mustn't hurt his father.

Bob Sparrow reviewed the rules. Every point would count for or against Caleb; most, his father assured him, would count against him. They rallied. The ball, a black blur, came off the front wall and at Caleb, reached his racquet, converted from a bullet to a whiffling bug, and returned by a more circuitous route, bumping into all the white walls. He scrambled up and back and nicked his left knee with his racquet, while his father seemed hardly to move from where he stood. His father let him serve first. He hit the ball overhead with all his might and lost sight of it. Returned, it deflected off a wall and dropped into a corner where Caleb would have needed a trowel to reach in and retrieve it. On every point his father shuffled in front of him, blocked his view, swatted balls past him, and dinked them into the front corners, forcing Caleb to thunder up the court, never in time.

After every slice and rifled crosscourt Caleb had to ask himself why it was that fathers and sons were so desperate to beat each other. (He had fallen two games behind.)

Why were they so often so angry with each other? For instance, given the opportunity, he would have swung at a ball and gladly connected instead with his old man's can. What mean-spirited thoughts to have about one's father. A moment later, stretching for a short shot, Caleb could do nothing but throw up a lob. His father, volleying from the T, drove the ball off the front wall and under Caleb's racquet. Caleb tried to jump up and back to avoid it, but was caught with gagging, nausea-inducing, knee-buckling pain. Surrender, that was his immediate reaction. Kneeling, he held himself and worked at just breathing and prayed he would be able to untie that crippling knot of pain which made moving, speaking, defending himself out of the question.

At last he coughed a few hoarse words. "Jesus, Dad, I'm just a beginner. Do you have to hit the ball quite so hard?"

"Smack in the family jewels, I take it."

"Don't talk about it! . . . That only makes it worse."

"Anything I can do for you?"

"You sound like a sales clerk."

"Damn it, Caleb, I'm trying to sound like your father. Would a drink of water help?"

Caleb said he would be okay.

"Now, Caleb, don't look at me that way. It was an accident."

Caleb didn't want to be like this man, his father. Then why were the alternatives to be better or be worse? Why couldn't he be comfortable with just being different? He recovered enough to continue the game. He lost four straight, but managed to retain his composure.

He wore the terrycloth robe to the shower. Bob Sparrow

47

led the way, his robe draped over his shoulders, everything about his backside ivory white and awobble.

"You're just a little wild out there. You flail at the ball." His father leaned into a shower stall to test the water.

"Now you tell me."

"Nobody takes criticism well on a squash court. Not enough space. Any swelling? Want me to look?"

"No, I don't want you to look. I'm fine."

"How's Bowie?" Beauregard's fraternity nickname.

"Busy."

"If you had told me thirty years ago that John Beauregard would do much more than play a good game of poker, I'd have laughed at you. Of course, you look at Paul Winchel at Kodak, Harold Foster at ABC, and Peter Kempton at Smith Barney and by God, the class hasn't done too badly for itself."

Caleb had decided that, relatively speaking, his own generation was young for its age. In their yearbook pictures his father's classmates looked older, more mannish than his own. It wasn't just that back then they wore their hair shorter and dressed more conservatively—their heads were bigger, their expressions more sober. But, growing up in the sixties and the seventies on a diet of turmoil, it was no wonder Caleb's generation showed stunted growth.

A spigot as big as a plate dumped heavy streams of water into Caleb's face and down his slippery body. He soaped joyously in that wealth of water. He caught a mouthful and blew a spout against the wall, the ordeal of the match behind him.

Bob Sparrow stuck his head in and looked Caleb up and down, as if to verify that all parts were intact and that this young version of himself could be relied upon some-day to bear the hereditary torch and family banner.

"Meet you in the lounge," he said.

The lounge adjoined the locker room. It was a big, warm, busy room with a bar, backgammon tables, and club chairs upholstered in slick black leather. Men of all ages, some in the club's blue bathrobe, others in towels, strolled in and out. They gulped booze and juices, gobbled peanuts, gnawed on candy bars, fudge brownies, and other delica-cies sent up in a dumbwaiter, cramming back into their systems whatever calories they had just worked off.

Caleb drank a mixture of grape juice and soda called a transfusion. It splashed into his empty stomach. Feeling the first contraction of a cramp in his right calf, he stretched his legs and leaned over to grab and bend back his toes.

Bob Sparrow slouched in a leather chair, his legs spread; his arms, when they weren't outstretched to wave or shake a hand, hung almost to the floor. Occasionally he would lift the squash racquet from his lap and grasp it in a fist like a scepter. A steady procession of members approached and paid their respects, like serfs swearing allegiance to their feudal lord. He asked after one man's wife, discussed the score of another's challenge match, and admired the zipper-stitched scar of a little man of cheerful disposition who had recently undergone a bypass operation.

"Elegant," said his father, a remark which induced such manic laughter that Caleb feared the stitches would tear before his eyes.

"I know executives who conduct most of their business here, breaking only for lunch and a nap in the library," said Bob Sparrow. "It may not be dignified, but it's effective. As a matter of fact, it was in this room, after old man Farshaw beat me three out of five in squash and took two hundred off me at backgammon, that he designated me his heir apparent."

Bob Sparrow raised his glass and drank deeply.

"I knew the promotion was coming, and I felt I'd earned it, but, still, I practically wept. This room has pleasant memories for me. I find that it's only when I'm in my club that I can believe in the brotherhood of man."

He continued in a whisper. "You won't find any queers in here either—the membership committee makes damned sure of that. And no scrubs. It goes without saying that you have to *be* somebody to belong. I think you should join here or the University Club. I have some weight with the membership committees."

"Let me think about it, Dad."

"I'm willing to pay the initiation fee and the first year's dues. In consulting, it's particularly advantageous to see and be seen. Of course I joined here because my father belonged."

In the darker corners of the lounge, voices were low, thick with intrigue: small gatherings of cavemen planning their next sortie, only here the plots were to topple CEOs or make killings in the market or seize cash-rich companies by proxy fights. They were not the elegant gentlemen Caleb had expected them to be—too rough and competitive. If by belonging to the club he would become one of them, he preferred to postpone his enlistment.

In the weeks which followed Caleb's lesson, no one at H&L invited him to play squash. If someone had, chances were he would have declined, citing a forthcoming dead-

line as an excuse. Omar Sahib tendered his resignation as
H&L team captain a week after his promotion to partner;
no one volunteered to replace him, and the team defaulted
its six remaining Corporate Challenge League matches.

5.

Cab Cabal

WHEN Caleb left work at 10 p.m. on the night of his birthday, executives on Park Avenue were still competing for cabs, straddling their briefcases, whistling and waving as an empty Checker plummeted out of the Helmsley Building tunnel and swerved toward the curb. One night Caleb saw an executive from ITT shove an officer from Bankers Trust in a dispute over a cab. They argued, grappled; their pinstripes crossed, and they toppled over. The ITT executive, the first to scramble to his feet, rolled his kneeling, wheezing opponent onto his back and place-kicked his briefcase into the street. The cab had disappeared, so, brushing his suit, he strode up Park Avenue, turning once to be sure that he was not followed. The banker sat on the curb and touched and squeezed his knees.

Only with a dial-a-cab voucher could an executive avoid arguments with his peers and claim a taxi as an inalienable right.

Caleb staked out a corner, too tired to walk east to Third Avenue where the cabs were more plentiful at that hour. He waited fifteen minutes, staring into the headlights of the oncoming traffic, raising and lowering his arm, until at last a cab broke ranks, bolted through a red light, and pulled up beside him. He swung the door open wide and, as though to underscore, for anyone watching, the justness of the universe, gently lowered himself in with a smile of self-assurance and satisfaction.

The cabby flipped him a piece of toffee wrapped in cellophane. The roof of the cab was covered with campaign buttons from presidential, gubernatorial, and forgotten local borough elections dating back to the Eisenhower administration. The candidates' names were printed in the red, white, and blue lettering of toothpaste cartons and patriotism. The cabby explained that after he became famous during the fifties for distributing his candies, every politician who cared a hoot for New York asked for the Candyman's endorsement.

"Hey, these politicians have been good to me. I got some citations glued on the dashboard here, and a couple of newspaper articles about me. So you can see I got some things to be thankful for. I liked La Guardia—best mayor we ever had. And after him, Lindsay. But Koch? No, sir. Koch is pro-business, no offense, and anti-union. Him with his upbringing, too."

They passed the stone pre-war building, green awning stretched taut to the curb, where Caleb's paternal grandmother had lived. For the last ten years of her life she had sat in that apartment with the drapes pulled, reading and rereading Virginia Woolf and Willa Cather until her death at eighty-two. Caleb remembered little about Simon Sparrow, his grandfather, one of the first experts on the aviation industry and a director of Pan American Airlines, except his hearing aid and the braided cord strung from a thick ear to the watch pocket of his vest. He'd written a thin volume entitled *Highways in the Sky: The Birth of the Aviation Industry*—a panegyric to the Wright Brothers' invention, which prophesied a day when airplanes would streak back and forth between continents, a great convenience for passengers who hadn't the stomach for seafaring or the leisure to cruise. Simon Sparrow was one person who would have appreciated the complexities of the Benefact Corp assignment.

When Caleb was a boy growing up in Westchester and someone mentioned the city, he thought of that Park Avenue apartment. On trips to visit their grandmother, the heavy iron-latticed doors of the building were held open for them by a polite doorman who ushered them past a vase of towering gladioli and down a narrow Persian carpet which halfway to the elevator rose and folded itself neatly over three short steps. Deep in the back of the building, where it smelled of varnish and must, they stepped into a mahogany elevator which carried them to the sixth floor. Robert rang the bell, and Caleb, his ear to the door, heard the faraway chimes. Inside was a best-behavior, hands-out-of-your-pockets, good-posture apartment. Caleb would skate in his socks over the dark hardwood floor, his hands behind his back like the skaters at Rockefeller Center, swinging from foot to foot and twirling. There was a great quiet in that apartment. Weary, he sat on a footrest and drank ginger ale. His grandmother, a tall woman who had lost none of her noble bearing in her old age, spoke to them in a surprisingly soft, hushed voice they could barely hear. The clock ticked; the ginger ale tingled in his nostrils.

At age seven Caleb thought of New York City as a gray place where people from the country lived during the winter and where men like his father performed their vague and nameless work. As Caleb understood it, his father's job was to see that there was plenty of food to fill the A&P and the Finast. He pictured his father spending his days scooping cereal into cereal boxes, and was surprised on visiting his father's office for the first time to see a tidy room with a metal desk and a square glass window and no sign of a cereal box. According to his mother, his father was in charge of the men who were in charge of putting the cereal into boxes. The cereal, she said, was in Minnesota.

During their teens Robert and Caleb began to associate New York with restaurants. After his divorce Bob Sparrow invited them in for weekends and took them out to dinner, offering a dollar to whichever of them came closest to guessing the cost of the meal. Robert, radicalized, brooded through these outings and once boldly accused his father of being materialistic. The charge went unanswered. Robert, Caleb noticed, pocketed the matchbook.

Caleb visited the city even less frequently during his college years; and yet this was when the myth of the city began to intrigue him. His flights from Columbus, Ohio, circled the island of Manhattan before landing at La Guardia, and below he saw, on the narrow spit of land moored to the continent by silver bridges, skyscrapers like outcroppings of quartz, opal, and agate. To build a sky-scraper seemed a glamorous and important and American thing for a man to do.

"Six trips to Bloomingdale's," said the cabby. "You'd think there was no other stores in this town. Must be a sale, that or some celebrity—you know, Elizabeth Taylor in the lingerie department. Should have asked. What do you do?"

"I work for a management consulting firm. We're hired by companies to tell them how to run their businesses."

"I bet they love that."

"Depends."

"You have to go to college to get a job like that?"

"Yes, you need credentials."

"I'm thinking of making a change. This line of work isn't what it used to be. During the day, just one big traffic jam. And Jesus are people nasty." Here he offered Caleb a fireball. "Take as much as you want—I can't get rid of the stuff. And I'm sick of hearing the Sugar Blues rap."

The toffee swallowed, Caleb accepted the fireball, pinched one end of the wrapper, and popped it into his mouth. Turning to stare out the window, he tucked it between his cheek and molars. He didn't feel he could recommend management consulting for everyone and said as much.

The cabby interrupted: "There goes another doctor."

Caleb felt the seat press against his back as the cab accelerated to draw even with a blue Mercedes bearing MD plates. The cabby honked the horn and shook his fist at the driver. In the flickering light a bespectacled driver looked over and gave the cabby the bird.

"Some of them recognize me now."

"What do you have against doctors?"

"Businessmen I can take; most of them don't make any bones about being out for the buck. But doctors—they've got a social responsibility."

The cabby had a constant drip of mucus down the back of his throat which his doctor told him came from an allergy.

"What am I allergic to? Mold, the doc says. Ever notice how it's always mold or dust or grass? That's because some mouse they fed the stuff to broke out in a rash."

For the next thirty blocks, Caleb, his mouth inflamed, listened to a treatise on adrenal glands and the shortcomings of the medical profession. He longed to get home.

6.

Thickly Settled

C A L E B had sublet a room in an apartment soon after he was offered a position at H&L.

He had spoken to some realtors and, to his dismay, discovered that unless he lived in Brooklyn or Queens or was willing to put his entire salary toward rent he could not afford to live alone. Finding a vacant Manhattan apartment promised to be as difficult as finding a job. Fortunately, after three weeks of calling friends, searching through classifieds in the *Times* and the *Village Voice*, and talking to a succession of ornery superintendents, Caleb heard of a room in a complex known as Yorkville Place. His source, an ex-classmate who knew the occupant, described the building as a luxury high-rise with a doorman, and the apartment as a spacious two-bedroom equipped with dishwasher and parquet wood floors—a terrific find which Caleb would be foolish not to take.

Dale Abernathy met Caleb at the door on a Saturday afternoon clad in a pair of red-checked boxer shorts. He made no effort to conceal his disappointment that Caleb was not a more prepossessing specimen, not, from outward appearances, a jock or potential skirt-chasing compatriot. Dale, originally from Rumsford, New Jersey, referred to himself as a Chemical Banker.

The apartment had one bathroom for two bedrooms, a living-room space with dining area on one side, and a narrow kitchen tiled in speckled yellow linoleum. In the living room a mustard-colored Castro convertible sofa bed faced a television set on a stool.

More than a little aware how snugly his shorts fit, Dale swaggered down the hall—the floor was admittedly parquet, but so badly scuffed as to make little difference—and, turning, threw out one arm to indicate the room.

"Willy couldn't get laid in New York, so he went back to Boston. Sorry it's such a mess." Dale twirled a Chap Stick cartridge in his fingers, removed the cap, and applied it to his lips.

"I heard you're at Hooker & Lyman. Does that mean you work to all hours of the morning? I'm a light sleeper, and I don't want the toilet flushing in the middle of the night."

In Caleb's opinion this Dale Abernathy was a bit uncouth; nevertheless, he decided to reserve judgment. He considered his generation's predisposition to make snap judgments one of its least attractive attributes. A little censorship of one's first reaction and a good second look was a more Christian way to behave.

Using the toe of his shoe, Caleb pushed aside a soiled white towel monogrammed "The Piping Rock Club." The room's single piece of furniture was a dirty mattress on its side, propped against the radiator. In an Alta poster taped to the wall, a goggled skier pummeled through a snow-laden pine forest. Caleb stepped over a Heineken bottle, an overturned ashtray, two issues of *Penthouse* magazine, a broken tube of Ultrabright toothpaste, a Wilson tennis-racquet cover, a can of Skoal, a balled pair of jockey shorts, a black silk cummerbund, a fly reel, and a dying spider plant in a cracked flower pot, the peat moss spilled on the cover of the *University of Vermont Alumni Bulletin*.

A window looked north over the sooty tenement roofs of Spanish Harlem. Caleb could see the twin towers and the cable loops of the George Washington Bridge.

"At night you get a great view. The girls love it," said Dale.

The room was affordable. Anxious to leave his father's apartment and be on his own, Caleb took it on the spot.

The night he moved in, Dale suggested they have a bite of dinner together; he canceled the plan only minutes later.

"Dredged up a date," he explained, fingering the Chap Stick applicator. "Manny Hanny trainee. They say she does the dance, if you follow my drift. Later."

He let the door slam behind him.

Yorkville Place was nicknamed "The Dorms." The three forty-story towers were originally part of a government-subsidized project on City land intended to provide needed low-income housing. However, upon their completion, they were rented out to nearly three thousand upwardly mobile, recent college graduates who found the location desirable and the now escalating rents still reasonable. Everyone under forty in the business world in Manhattan knew someone who lived there, and those who did live there knew countless others in identical suites above and below them. They had met during spring vacation in Bermuda or while waiting tables at the Harborside on Martha's Vineyard; they had crewed on the *Windjammer* during the New York Yacht Club cruise or ushered at the Westchester Cotillion; or they belonged to St. Bart's, the Bath and Tennis Club, or the Junior League.

The sparsely furnished lobby resembled the lobby of the Reeves Building. Heels clicked over shiny floors. Electric doors whooshed open and shut. A walkie-talkie sputtered static on the belt of the security guard who peered into video consoles or spoke into the wall of intercoms, announcing arrivals.

Caleb checked his mailbox and joined a small congregation at the elevator banks staring up expectantly at the lit monitor, awaiting, he realized, no greater visitation, no greater transcendence, than the Otis Elevator Company could provide.

Entering his apartment, he found Dale snoozing on the Castro, his shoes and briefcase on the floor beside him. An onion smell of dirty socks hung in the air. The television gave a squeal of laughter.

In his pile of mail, tossed on the kitchen counter, American Express had sent him his bill along with a glossy pamphlet advertising a limited-edition porcelain cougar, a gold Rolex watch, and an attaché-size home computer, all of which could be ordered by mail. He opened a birthday card from his mother in which a cartoon character made a sexual innuendo about age and potency. He shook the envelope. A check (for twenty-five, he guessed) fluttered toward the floor, looped, and was caught at the knees. Ruth Ross had sent him an invitation to a party later that week. And there was a letter from his brother, Robert, postmarked June 4, Santa Barbara, California.

Although he professed to be amused by Robert's career path, Caleb was secretly proud of him for going off on his own and devoting his life to a cause he believed in. He saw in Robert his father's stubbornness and will, but tempered by a generous nature and a quiet dignity. He tore open the envelope and removed a card, "The Savior," depicting a comely, bearded Christ crowned with thorns.

DEAR CALEB,

I know what you're thinking. You're thinking that your brother is writing to give you a hard time about following in the old man's footsteps and working in big business. Well I'm not and I won't. You are twenty-four (happy birthday, kid!) and know your own mind and what you want out of life. Nothing I might say could make a difference.

I'll admit that Dad and his Olympus Brands still drive me nuts. I can't believe he feels he is doing anything worthwhile for this country pushing all that junk food on the public. I can't make him realize that people wouldn't buy that garbage if there was readily available, inexpensive nutritious food on the market.

I do hear Olympus treats its employees well which is worth something.

It's not hard for me to picture you strolling down the avenues in a three-piece suit, swinging your brief-case. I bet you are quite the sophisticate!

The real reason I am writing, aside from sending birthday greetings, is to announce—and you are the first to hear the news—my engagement. Sounds strange, doesn't it? I used to think of marriage as one more hopelessly outmoded social convention. In a societal context I suppose I still do. God knows the folks didn't make much of a go of it. However, in the context of the church, I believe it is different. I am in love with a fellow member of The Wave, a lovely woman by the name of Clare Fleur (Bright Flower!). She is in love with me, and we believe it is God's will that we be married. The wedding will be held here in August. Hope you can attend. We are, needless to say, very happy.

Please keep the secret until I can write to Mom and Dad. They should hear it from the "Jesus Freak's" mouth. I sincerely wish you continued success. More info on the wedding to follow.

God bless you,
ROBERT

Caleb folded the letter and returned it to its envelope and gave a low whistle. He should have expected the an-nouncement, he decided. Robert's pursuit of alternative life styles and sojourn against conformity, provided they were to end well, could not be sustained alone. He needed company.

The church, which had begun as a religious commune, had opened branches all over California. An immensely successful advertising campaign stressing proximity to God and nature, modern facilities including indoor pool, Jacuzzi, fitness courses, and a health-food cafeteria, had boosted membership until the church now competed favorably with Reverend Sun Myung Moon's Unification Church. For the past three years Robert had lived at the Santa Barbara branch. He had been chosen to serve on the Quality of Life Committee, and all indications were that he would soon be invited to chair it.

This news would delight their mother, whose faith in the institution of marriage was mammoth. Periodically she sent Caleb wedding announcements neatly clipped from the "Social Announcements" page of the Sunday *Times*—what she referred to as "the ladies' sports pages." Daughters of her Westchester friends were getting married, weekly it seemed, to men from Merrill Lynch, the Morgan Bank, and Cravath Swaine & Moore. The good brides, she wrote, were getting away; she hoped he would act soon and get down to the real business of living, which Caleb translated to read: raising kids and falling into debt.

She overlooked completely the fact that her own first marriage had ended badly. The divorce had occurred long before Bob Sparrow's promotion to the presidency of Olympus Brands, the day his "ship came in."

Caleb was never entirely sure what caused the divorce— both his parents were mum on the subject. Robert and he came up with a sketchy reconstruction of events like an artist's rendering of a courtroom drama.

In the early seventies Jane Sparrow began to take lessons in pottery and batik. These hobbies embarrassed Bob Sparrow, whose only concessions to the times were flairs in his trousers and a dozen wide, flower-print neckties from Bloomingdales, which he loathed. He apparently mistook her growing disenchantment with their suburban life style for a fad. When he complained that she was not supportive enough, that she showed no interest in his career, she admitted that she found his work and his friends tiresome. A separation followed. Jane Sparrow spent a month in Japan studying pottery, and on her return he sought a reconciliation, offering to change his habits, to take her on a world tour, to grow a beard. She was unmoved. Finally, he let her go. She sold the house in Katonah, and for the next few months, Robert, Caleb, and she, living a gypsy existence, meandered through New England in her Country Squire station wagon in search of prep schools for her boys. Caleb was thirteen and he remembered that trip vividly. Robert was feuding with their mother or staring out the window, stonily silent; Caleb himself had indigestion from too many plates of French fries. In the end, Jane Sparrow found homes for the homeless. A year later she married Rupert Shaw, the Mannes Academy headmaster.

Robert's conversion had been one of the great disappointments of Jane Shaw's life. She had hoped he would be a college professor. When asked what Robert did, she felt she saved time by describing him as a Catholic priest.

Caleb removed his tie and belt, unbuttoned his trousers,

which made it easier to breathe, and mulled over whether or not to exercise. He had put on some weight since joining H&L—not in any one place, but detectable just the same—and unless he exercised after work he felt lethargic all evening. Dale had talked him into a one-month trial membership at a local health club with pool and Universal Gym. During Caleb's first visit an instructor, groaning and blowing, demonstrated the Universal machines. He advised Caleb to admire himself in the mirrors. "Tell yourself what a tough dude you are. It all helps." Examining his biceps at the end of the first week and noting with wan amusement his lack of progress—not one new muscle had sprouted along those narrow tendons—he decided to forfeit the remaining three weeks. The next afternoon he purchased a pair of tire-treaded running sneakers and took up jogging instead.

It was too late to jog unless he wished to risk being mugged. At dusk recently one of Grayson's friends, an IBM salesman, had been grabbed by marauders and thrown up against the chain-link fence surrounding the black waters of the Central Park reservoir; now his hair was turning prematurely gray.

The alternative to jogging was to do calisthenics on the living-room floor—there was no space in his room. Caleb decided against them since they would wake Dale.

He lowered the volume of the television. Dale, head thrown back, mouth open, breathed hoarsely. Every so often a breath caught on his epiglottis and clogged a valve. He would swallow, wet his mouth with a cud-chewing noise, and resume breathing. A mouth breather—no wonder his lips chapped.

Dale was resting up for his late-night excursion to the Third Avenue singles bar, where, after a year in the city, he knew the bouncers, bartenders, and regulars well enough to feel at home. By contrast, Caleb's social life was in its infancy.

He had dated Linda, a bored senior at NYU who confided to him in the first hour of their date that she was a vegetarian. Along with meat, she had apparently given up movies, too, and insisted on leaving Hitchcock's *Rear Window* even before they saw the director's cameo. He didn't call her again. He met Sally Happer on a booze cruise sponsored by a socially aggressive group of Southern women, recent arrivals in New York, all hungry for night life and wealthy Northern spouses. Before the Circle Line reached the Statue of Liberty he had told her much of what there was to know about himself and was attempting to convince her—he had already picked up a bit of her drawl —that there was such a thing as love at first sight. When they met for dinner three days later, he was disappointed by her new pixie haircut, her pink Shetland sweater and knee-length skirt, her way of characterizing people as "neat" and "precious." He made no further mention of love, and watching her work her way through lamb chops and a piece of chocolate marble cheesecake and swell before his eyes, he swore to exercise more caution if he ever again fell for a Southerner on a booze cruise. He had dated Trish Grumlach-Bunschu, who, after explaining her ethnic heritage (Russian, Polish, Dutch, and German), remarked, "I know what you think. You think I'm a mutt." He drank anisette with Emily Bradford after his mother, a friend of her mother, bullied him into calling her. Emily didn't like the fact that he lived uptown, that he didn't "create," that he showed no sensitivity to the controversy over nuclear weapons. She ruled him out as a prospective friend or lover. Sandra, Grayson's half-sister, talked forever about her boyfriends, extolling their virtues and the material and spiritual sacrifices they had made on her behalf. When she noticed him staring at her legs, she said, "I have good calves, don't I? Admit you'd like to bite them."

Caleb had read an ad for *Metropolitan Magazine* which summed up the urban woman:

When people ask me whether I dress to please men or other women, I think they are as silly as people who ask whether I dream in color or black and white (color, of course, since life itself *is in color). I dress to please me—some innate feeling of how I want to present myself. My favorite magazine says viva fashion, viva my pleasure in it, and shows me the most exciting clothes to inspire me. I love that magazine. I guess you could say I'm that Metropolitan Girl!*

This was just the kind of woman to avoid, the kind who would spend his every last dime in Bendel's, who would insist on a mink coat and a maid during the first year of marriage, who would do her damnedest to convert him into That Metropolitan Boy and have him marching to work hailing fellow pedestrians, "Viva la job! Viva la promotion!"

These women were not his sort. Just which metropolitan women were, he had yet to decide; his job allowed him few weekends to do the necessary research.

The New York men were no easier to understand than

the women. In the transition from high school to college, they had, of choice, become types: those who wanted to be lawyers changed the frames of their glasses to tortoise shell, the future academics grew beards, and the soon-to-be executives bought suits. But now that they were out of college such behavior was less a posture than a conviction. They were career-oriented. They grabbed for high-paying jobs, coveted automobiles, spoke of houses in the country. Caleb, still a newcomer to this corps, envied them their complacency and the grand faith they had in their own destinies.

He sat at the kitchen counter and ate cold cuts from the local delicatessen spread neatly on white bread, the same meal he ate every night. He washed it down with Rolling Rock.

In some respects it was just as well he had had no steady girlfriend during his first few months at H&L; he was busy enough as it was. His one serious college romance had left him feeling it was a whole lot easier and more fun to be single. Amy Hoagland—she had a 4.0 average. She said her family was in the *Guinness Book of World Records* for most divorces. Sometimes she accused him of being too practical and too literal-minded and too serious; he countered with allegations of irrationality and evasiveness. They fell in and out of love over the course of their junior year. Her moods astonished him. One day she wanted to see if they could hold hands for twelve straight hours, and the next day she scurried around his dorm suite looking for her lost pocketbook, pushed over a chair, and yelled at him: "You are mild-mannered, Caleb. Did you know that? Mild-mannered!" When, fatigued, he finally broke the relationship off, she sat on her trundle bed in her bathrobe emitting little gasps and burps; he felt vicious, criminal. He was in no hurry to repeat the experience.

Caleb opened another Rolling Rock. The phone rang and he grabbed it on the first ring. A Denison classmate invited him to a seminar entitled "The Power of Acknowledgment." Caleb explained that he had other commitments, and tried to decline politely. The classmate, who had lost his job some months before when the magazine which had hired him folded, grew defensive. He accused Caleb of dismissing the seminar as a gimmick, like est or TM, which it wasn't. He had been skeptical at first, too, but, there was no question in his mind that it had improved his outlook on life. When Caleb assured him that he took the idea seriously but did in fact have commitments, the classmate hung up on him.

Caleb still expected a birthday call from his mother. He saw little of her now that he lived in New York. Rupert Shaw, a gigantic New Englander with the righteousness of a chaplain and the crew cut of a marine, made Caleb uncomfortable. He had spent Thanksgiving with them last year. The Mannes Academy campus, with its maple-shaded drive, flat, drab playing fields, quadrangle of crisscrossing footpaths and red brick dormitories, had a scruffy look about it as though the alumni were somewhat stingy in their Annual Giving. The school had a reputation for being exceedingly strict, and the all-male student body was adept at parade marching. Shaw's toast during the meal touched on the forefathers, U.S. vulnerability to Soviet first-strike capability, the decline of the church in American life, and ended with a plea for improved high-school reading scores.

Afterward, as Caleb helped to load the dishes into the washer, Shaw pulled out the Phi Beta Kappa key he wore on his watch chain and swung it as if to hypnotize. "Here is something your father doesn't have."

Before climbing into bed that night, a squeaky double-bed box spring and camphor-smelling mattress which he had bought for forty dollars in college after he began to date Amy Hoagland, Caleb sprayed the floor around the bed with roach repellent. He kept Samuelson's *Economics* on the nightstand as a further defense.

He stood at the window in his jockey shorts. At eleven o'clock the cable lights on the George Washington Bridge went out, and all that could be seen of the bridge was the taut string of white lights along the ramp. Overhead, sets of blinking red and green lights sank from the sky and descended into La Guardia, jets propelled by Hegel Penguin engines.

The intercom buzzer woke Caleb at 2 a.m. When he answered, a man's voice demanded that his hat be returned. If it wasn't returned, the voice threatened to set fire to the building.

"Hat?" said Caleb.

"It's a Stetson."

"Oh, the Stetson." Caleb, containing his fury, said he was sorry, partner, but it fit, and he had every intention of keeping it—for good. And, for his information, the police were on the way. Caleb staggered back to bed. Where was the doorman, and why hadn't the Texan been evicted? He shouldn't have to put up with such disturbances living in a luxury high-rise.

In bed again, he could hear noises from Dale's room, the same noises heard off and on since Caleb first moved into the apartment: feline cries, hard gasps of exertion, and, once, a soft, childlike whine. He pushed a pillow against the threshold of the door to help seal out the sound and, wide awake, bit the corner of his mattress until his teeth ached.

7.

Century Runs

Bird-watching had begun as a hobby for Caleb at age nine when he received a jigsaw puzzle of American songbirds for Christmas. During a snowy day in January he assembled it on a card table set up before the fireplace, and learned the names of birds as he searched for the pieces to fit the towhee's rufous side, the cardinal's crest, the cutter bill of the evening grosbeak, and the eye ring of the ruby-crowned kinglet. By spring and the onset of migration he could distinguish the sexes of the sparrows and finches nervy enough to visit the birdfeeder nailed to a plank outside the kitchen window. He had hung other feeders, too: wire mesh for suet, a pair of dangling shacks with perches for communal feeding, and a tubular contraption designed for chickadees. The backyard was a mall of birdfeeders.

On the day the first warblers arrived, he borrowed his father's binoculars and tiptoed through the Ward Pound Ridge Reservation, stopping to watch and listen. Three years and countless walks later, dawn walks and owl walks and walks along canals and around reservoirs and through pine forests and along seashores, his life list had grown to 400 of the 445 species present in Eastern U.S., omitting hybrids, subspecies, strays, and accidentals. In many instances he had searched a bird's natural habitat periodically over the course of a week, imitating its call by whistling or wetly kissing the back of his hand. If he was lucky, the bird would eventually appear on a limb overhead, watching him—a gnatcatcher—hopping, hyperactive, until a sudden movement or a snap of a twig underfoot sent it diving into a thicket. When he found a bird on a roadside, an indigo bunting or a scarlet tanager, the neck broken but otherwise a perfect specimen, he would stroke the breast down and draw out the wing by its wrist to admire the primary and secondary feathers, the scapulars and the axillars.

He had completed two "century runs" in which he sighted over a hundred species in a single day. Half of these he had been able to identify by their calls alone. While visiting friends on the coast of Maine, his sighting of a yellow-nosed albatross, unmistakable for its seven-foot span of saberlike wings, earned him a write-up in the Audubon newsletter. He was described as a tenacious young ornithologist whose life ambition was to spot an ivory-billed woodpecker in the Big Thicket of Eastern

Texas, and to have a hybrid named after him (Sparrow's sparrow was their prediction). The following fall, before his parents' separation, Arnold Denmark, the renowned Boston ornithologist, invited him to go birding on Cape Cod, an honor his mother declined for him, citing the expense involved and the potential conflict with his schoolwork. On that matter his parents were agreed; they were not going to encourage his bird-watching.

Today, in the city, the few birds he saw with any frequency were rock doves: pigeons. All other species were strays and accidentals, travelers grounded by bad weather or tourists like the cardinal in May he saw perched on a curb and which, at first, he mistook for a candy wrapper. The pigeons were the permanent residents. They flew in their lofty, circular, swooping formations, roosted on the same ledges day after day, clucked and cooed their contentment.

8.

Running Numbers

FIVE days a week, at 6:30 a.m., Caleb's alarm clock chirped its electric birdcall into the cave of his sleep. Invariably his arms were wedged under his pillow and his legs refused to withdraw from their pockets of warm mattress. He extricated one hand and reset the alarm for 7:15, aware this meant competition for the shower and the perils of commuting at rush hour, but he was asleep again before his good sense could put up much of a fight. Later the sudden spit and rush of steam and water, the spattering of spray on the plastic shower curtain, and the morning noises of his roommate woke him. He heaved his long, foreign-feeling body out of bed and yawned. The barefoot march to the kitchen, during which he shucked off the husks of sleep, was one of the most torturous acts of the day. He filled a saucepan with water and dropped in two eggs and placed the pan over a flame.

On a recent morning a glass pitcher full of Welch's grape juice had slipped out of his hands. Staring at the purple pool, he realized how much freedom he had lost since college. The pattern of working and sleeping, and the even more regular habits of his bowels, were only infrequently interrupted, and then by mishaps or a birthday which made him conscious of a vague dissatisfaction and sometimes a prickling apprehension that he was forgetting an important appointment. On such occasions, when he saw how regulated his life had become, he would fall into a dark mood and not speak unless spoken to, and then only grumpily.

A day later he'd had trouble with the toilet.

He was in the kitchen when Dale appeared nude in the living room, toweling himself dry, and got down on his hands and knees and crawled across the floor until he found the phone. He withdrew it from under the couch by the cord, hand over hand. When his secretary answered, he sat back on his haunches in a posture which must have been painful, and explained that he was at the dentist having his teeth cleaned, would be in midmorning. Could she turn on his desk lamp and scatter some papers around so it looked as if he had stepped away for a moment? She got the idea. He thanked her, blew her a kiss over the phone, and as Caleb stepped into the shower he heard Dale's door close, followed by voices on the *Today* show. Dale rarely spoke

77

about his work at the bank, but rumor had it he had almost been fired from the training program for overdrawing his NOW account.

Caleb's ablutions that particular morning would have gone according to plan if it had not been for the toilet, which, when flushed, began to fill gradually until the fluids swirled near the rim of the bowl. He lifted the lid. Nothing appeared to be wrong, so, after a moment of deliberation in which he realized he was already late for work, he flushed again. The toilet promptly regurgitated gallons of water onto the tile floor. A flood spread across the hall and through his bedroom door. He snatched the towels off the racks, even his bathrobe, to dam the flow. To this pile he added the small amount of toilet paper that remained on the roll. His foot-stomping brought Dale into the hall.

"That's my towel."

"Dale, I think if you used less toilet paper, this wouldn't have happened." Caleb, breathing heavily, said this as nicely as he could.

"Do you want to know what makes that happen? Rats. There was probably a rat in the pipes, on his way from 19A to 20A, when you just happened to flush, and now he's wedged in there, probably drowning, too. Maybe it's a good thing this happened. I don't want rats in the apartment. We've got enough problems with roaches."

"Are you going to stand there or are you going to help?"

"Hey, pal, I wasn't the last one who flushed it."

Caleb shoveled up the soggy pile with the handle of the broom and dumped it, dripping, into the bathtub. The water level in the toilet sank, drained, and left the bowl dry. He restrained the impulse to flush once more.

That incident ranked as the domestic adventure of the month.

Within a week of joining H&L, Caleb had bought his first three-piece suit, a navy-blue pinstripe, off the rack of S. K. Friedman's for $120. The alterations, free, were finished a few days later, and he carried the flat box home under one arm, his adrenaline running at the thought of the blue wool, the slender, white stripes, the way the suit hugged his chest and squared his shoulders. In his room he undressed hastily, dropping articles of clothing in a semicircle around him. He knew the suit fit, he had stood before the mirror at Friedman's until the tailor groused at him. Now he wanted to see once more how the cuffs broke on his shoes, how in his normal posture the sleeves reached to the heel of his palm. He pulled at the lapels, buttoned and unbuttoned the jacket, preened before the mirror. The look was right: urbane. Let his sideburns gray, let his chin double, the effect could not be spoiled. He felt for the first time that he had indeed entered his middle age, that placid expanse of undifferentiated years where life continually improved. Here was the payoff for those sixteen years of education—the opportunity to look right, by which he meant professional, and to be comfortable and respected. When he sat on the bed, the vest crumpled at the waist and the pants legs retreated up his calves, revealing white ankles which looked like birch limbs shoved into his shoes. He noticed another thing, too: the wool, a handsome but coarse grade, scratched. Boxer shorts would remedy that. The suit was nice, just not a particularly good suit for sitting in.

Seven months later, after more expensive trips to Barney's and J. Press, he thought of his suits as second skins. In the mornings he dressed mechanically and, more often than not, put on what he had worn the day before. Wary of leaving valuables around, he hid his checkbook under his pillow and his gold tie clips in the spider plant. He would run his boiled eggs under cold water and pocket them to eat during the walk to the 86th Street subway station.

That June an early heat wave baked the streets and warmed the subway tunnels until the air underground was moist and shimmery, alive with odors of exhaust and tar and perspiration. He stood on the express train to Grand Central, hot, crammed against other commuters, holding up the *Wall Street Journal* folded to the width of a paperback, narrow columns of print joggling before his eyes. Every day he crossed the lobby of Grand Central, an ocean of people fed by three major tributaries: the subways, trains, and street. Shoulders might bump or briefcases collide, but no blows were ever exchanged. Yet Caleb, emerging at the other end and stepping onto the escalator which carried him up like precious cargo, gracefully, silently, into the lobby of the Pan Am Building, always felt that a needless battle had been waged and feebly won. He swore to leave earlier the next morning to avoid the crowd.

As he passed the plate-glass window of La Trattoria restaurant, he would see his lean profile reflected and ask himself why it was he still bounced when he walked. His arches pitched him up, not forward, and his free arm did too much work in a swing like a short crawl stroke. His walk was conspicuous, lanky and exuberant, which he didn't mind except that the firm preferred to have its employees blend with their surroundings. This was a small but important part of the firm's concept of professional deportment. In fact, so serious was H&L about the appearance and conduct of its professional staff that the firm paid to have all new members sent to "charm school"—a weekend at a conference center in Atlanta where they could be drilled in protocol, team dynamics, interviewing techniques, and the firm's dot-and-dash-point writing style.

Between sumptuous meals of roast duck, veal, and sirloin, the "rookies" were coached in etiquette. ("Carry your briefcase in your left hand. This keeps your right hand free for handshaking. Stand straight, never bend the knees. And be firm when you shake. Let's practice.") As an exercise in communications skills they were led out onto the lawn, blindfolded, and given an L. L. Bean tent to assemble. The lifeguard taught them how to bob in the swimming pool with their hands tied behind their backs, in the event they were ever bound and thrown off an ocean liner in the course of a consulting assignment. There were mandatory lessons in the Heimlich maneuver because an H&L client had choked to death during a business luncheon and the account was lost. Yoga was offered to those who wished to combat stress and improve concentration. Caleb even sat in on a karate class, where the instructor, a black belt, demonstrated a self-defense tactic known as the Delayed Death Touch.

Most useful were the interview drills. Here the rookies took turns interviewing each other before a videotape machine. Then Tony Graves of the New York office replayed the interviews and critiqued them. Caleb learned the eight procedural steps to a successful client interview:

1. Make eye contact to establish honesty and credibility.
2. Put the interviewee at ease.
3. Determine the purpose and scope of the interview.
4. Begin with open-ended questions.
5. Keep pad and pencil in plain view and make no secret of note-taking.
6. Avoid unnecessary or distracting movements, i.e., drumming fingers, tapping foot.
7. Paraphrase what you have been told.
8. Thank the interviewee for his/her precious time.

Graves recommended they put down their pencils during particularly sensitive questions to give the illusion that a response would be off the record. ("Is there anything you would like to tell me about the production problems in your division?")

At the end of the weekend the rookies were asked to appraise the program's effectiveness and rate the various events. On one subject there was unanimity: the food, which had been excellent.

Caleb arrived at work late on Tuesday morning. Pike had left two notes on his desk. The first, written at 8:15, read, "Where are you?" and the second, at 8:45, "By now Henry Ford would have split your desk into kindling and hired a replacement. My patience borders on saintliness."

Pike tipped a cigar ash into a Styrofoam cup. "Ah, Mr. Sparrow, thought you'd take breakfast in bed this morning, did you? Kind of you to join us. What's the prognosis? Finished?"

Pike was as taut and smooth in dress and manner as a freshly made bed. A workaholic, he was in the office seven days a week without exception. He liked to boast about his intelligence: how in college he had impressed Blaine, the famous business professor at Stanford—father of the science of Organizational Behavior—and was promptly offered a teaching fellowship, or how Stanley Kaplan, convinced Pike could score an 800 on the Graduate Management Aptitude Test, had urged Pike to take his course tuition-free in return for an endorsement. Pike did score an 800, without the benefit of the course. Then he had gone on to business school at the University of Chicago, where he was second in his class.

Every now and then he invited to lunch a subordinate whose work he considered particularly disgraceful. There, while they ate, he read the damning job-end appraisal, thanked the consultant or researcher for his contribution to the firm, and severed his livelihood with two or three quick machete-like sentences. This had been the fate of Penny Singleton. The next day he was penitent and re-morseful, and sat with his feet on the radiator in his office, staring out the window. Like a boa constrictor, he had to rest and digest—the deed still bulged in his throat. Before long he was back to normal, dragging Caleb, Penny's re-placement, with him to Paul Stuart, where he asked Caleb's opinion on the choice of fabrics and ordered a dozen custom-made shirts.

On one such trip he took Caleb into his confidence.

"I consider you a nice person, Caleb, and myself—in

some respects—a mean person. That's the basic difference between us. I keep thinking my not being a nice person has to do with the way my parents raised me. That if they'd given me more affection when I was a child, I'd be a better person. It's true what they say about Jewish parents: they push their kids."

"I think who you are depends on your environment."

"You mean if I'd gone to college out in the Midwest the way you did, some of that heartland wholesomeness would have rubbed off on me?"

"You needn't go to such extremes."

"But you think people can change?"

"You don't?"

"For the better? I can't think of anyone who did."

He had a high, jerky laugh and a fondness for rumor and innuendo. If one fell into his good graces, which happened only to those willing, or at least able, to tolerate his hazing, temper tantrums, and perfectionism, he shared his insights into the sexual proclivities of H&L professionals: Miller, the Managing Partner of the New York office, was screwing a consultant during lunch hours; and Hanson, a principal whom Pike considered an arch-rival, was queer. But if there had been an H&L necktie, Pike would have worn it. He seemed to like Caleb and in his first review had commented favorably on Caleb's social development within the firm: "From an initial demeanor of reticence and shyness, Caleb has developed a sense of humor as well as an interpersonal style which is appropriately tough." Pike drew on his morning cigar as he looked at Caleb and listened. They were printing the first draft of the report.

Caleb explained to Pike that they were in line behind the Allied project.

"This is what you do," said Pike, emitting smoke. "Tell Linda to give your copy the highest priority, and I don't just mean 'rush.' I want the report, what we've got of it, on my desk by tomorrow morning. Tell her you're holding her personally accountable—some words to that effect. She'll understand. And this takes precedence over any of that Allied crap the Tech Group is doing. That's an encyclopedia they're writing, and if we get stuck behind it, we're goners. Come on, Caleb! Can't you even pretend you're having a good time?"

Caleb promised to try.

"Off, Sparrow! You have your orders. Flutter away."

"If it isn't one of the walking wounded," said Jamie Ordway.

"Why don't you ever have anything nice to say?" Caleb mumbled, feeling persecuted.

"Why don't you ever buy me flowers, or lunch?"

Jamie Ordway was an overqualified researchers' secretary. She had helped to found the first sorority at her college, an achievement which received high play on her résumé. She had been at the firm two years and knew more about its workings and the established bureaucratic channels than many of the partners, and was on a first-name basis with everyone from the kitchen steward to the partners. Pike maintained that if she were only a more competent typist—she showed a flagrant disregard for margins and spelling, and in one embarrassing communiqué Exxon lost an "x"—she would have been promoted. She talked about leaving the firm to join Macy's as an assistant buyer, where she wouldn't have to type. She had a friend there in the lamp department who loved it. Of course such jobs weren't easy to come by. Caleb suspected that, despite her grumblings, she enjoyed her status at H&L. She sat erect at one end of a row of secretaries, busy but not pressured, eligible for overtime, privy to hall conversations and insiders' information about the seasonal hiring and firing of H&L staff.

"I thought you considered that stuff unprofessional. Besides, Grayson might get the wrong idea."

Straight black hair, blue eyes, a gentle mouth, and an ex-swimmer's long torso and strong legs, she was attractive and jockish. Grayson, she had informed Caleb one day, swearing him to secrecy, had a crush on her and took her to lunch on the sly. Caleb admired him that much more. On top of everything else, Grayson had found romance, and within twenty feet of his desk. The fact that it was a clandestine romance made it all the more interesting and enviable.

"Flimsy excuse. I think you're just selfish."

"Busy."

"Selfish."

"There you go again. I have enough problems without having a rude secretary."

"Rude? Caleb, you can go to hell!" She threw a box of paper clips at him, which burst into a rain of silver slivers.

"That's just great, Jamie." Caleb squatted to scrape the clips into a pile.

"Next time it'll be my paperweight."

The day was under way and Caleb was speed-walking

through the firm. His first assignment at H&L had been a strategic plan for a forest-products company. Knowing little of accounting or finance, he had humbled himself to ask regrettably simplistic questions, and sacrificed his evenings and weekends to complete work the other researchers could finesse in a matter of hours. To keep himself from panicking as he walked through the firm, he had whispered to himself that he was promising and enterprising and that he belonged there. Within a week he could find his way through the narrow stacks of the research library, and knew how to use *Value Line*, the *Dun & Bradstreet Directory of Corporate Officers*, and the *Directory of Associations*. He was even adept at fixing paper jams in the Xerox machine.

A consulting assignment, he soon realized, never ended. Once hired by the company, the consulting firm was forever its maid and errand boy. The details of implementation often lasted months after the study team had disbanded and the client had received a final bill. Questions had to be answered, letters written, extra copies of the report run off. All these tasks were delegated to the junior member of the team, usually a researcher who watched them pile up faster than he could possibly complete them. Of necessity, many were discreetly shelved and forgotten.

Linda gave the text pages to the micom operator Danny McGraw, a failed pianist who wore rings on every finger. He could type 110 words a minute, his hands dancing over the keyboard, his delivery near perfect.

"Don't let those Allied folks give you any work, Danny."

Danny pushed back his chair and crossed his arms. "I have nightmares about Allied. Those heathens on the project work me until I have blisters on my fingers. They've

87

written a tome the size of the King James Bible and equally unreadable. 'Farm it out,' says Linda. 'No, we would rather have Danny do it. He understands our needs.' They only want me because then the typing stays in-house and all they have to do to correct something is walk upstairs. If I'm such a precious team asset, why don't they hire me, or cut me in for a percentage of the profits, or even just tip me, for pity's sake?"

"You wouldn't be in demand if you weren't so good."

"You're too kind for this business, Caleb. And I shouldn't complain. How's your social life?"

"Mediocre."

"Take some time off, Caleb, and go to the beach. These are your salad days. Be a shame to waste them."

On his way back to his desk Caleb found a pink slip in his message box from a Mr. Tapolletti, Vice President of United Chicago Industries.

In order to make recommendations for Benefact Corp which would be consistent with industry practice and, therefore, fair and agreeable to the Board and the stockholders, H&L had to know how much other companies were paying their top executives and how prevalent and lucrative were their benefit packages. To get this information Pike had asked Caleb to perform a survey. Briefed on what questions to ask, what data to gather, Caleb had called the twenty largest aerospace and manufacturing companies which most resembled Benefact Corp in size and lines of business.

The responses were varied:

"Shouldn't we get paid something for participating?"

"You want *me* to tell *you* what I make?"

"We feel, given our recent merger with United Technologies, that our data, assuming it were available, would not be applicable to your study."

"He's on vacation."

"$230,000 last year with another $100,000 incentive comp. Not too bad, would you say? And I'd love to know what those other bums get paid."

"Put it in writing."

"Not nearly enough. No, my friend, not nearly enough."

"I don't do business with Benefact Corp and you can tell that egomaniac Jack Ransome I said so."

Mr. Tapolletti was one of fourteen executives who had provided data. A gruff man who purported to be nobody's fool, he was later convinced he had been swindled. Now he demanded the survey results. He let Caleb know in blistering Southside Chicago language what he thought of H&L and its questionable business practices.

"Selling it to the press, aren't you, Sparrow? I'm no dummy. We got lawyers. That's one thing we got plenty of in this company. You get those figures to me, or I'm going to pull one of my Harvard Law School lawyers out of our legal department, one with plenty of litigation experience, and see what he thinks. By the way, in case you are interested, I'm taping this conversation."

Caleb offered to transfer the call to Pike or Beauregard, but Tapolletti preferred to deal strictly with Caleb, young and green enough to appreciate his formidable gifts of persuasion. Caleb explained that Mr. Tapolletti would just have to be patient—the first regressions had been run the day before, and the participants' reports would be at least a week in preparation. Mr. Tapolletti had to appreciate the amount of work which went into this kind of study. No, said Mr. Tapolletti, Hooker & Lyman had to realize that Vincent Tapolletti was mighty tired of the run-around. He hung up on Caleb.

The office was air-conditioned, but on hot days the narrow researchers' room, lacking adequate ventilation, grew warm and humid. Grayson and Caleb had bought fans, which whirred and gently peeled papers off their desks and floated them to the floor. The fans stirred up the air and cooled their perspiration. Caleb drank three cups of coffee and two cans of Tab a day and was still thirsty.

Outside, a wind picked up and the building gently swayed, not enough so that Caleb could feel it, but enough so the walls in the room creaked.

He began a new regression analysis, and for a time his calculator and the creaking walls harmonized: click, click, click, creak; click, click, click, creak. Then a shout and footsteps. Grayson threw open the door to the researchers' room and charged in, breathless.

"They're evacuating the building! There's been a bomb threat."

"Is this a joke?" An alarm sounded and Caleb scrambled up from his chair.

"What should I take?"

"Leave everything."

Caleb put his calculator in his pocket.

In the halls a line of H&L employees hurried toward the fire exits. Grayson and Caleb waited for Jamie to put the vinyl cover over her IBM Correcting Selectric III typewriter and lock her desk. As a group they funneled into the crowded stairwell and began the twenty-five-flight descent to the street.

Jamie cursed her clogs.

"Serves you right," said Grayson.

"He can't stand my posturepedic clogs," said Jamie. "Not dignified enough. But my brother works for Dr. Scholl's, so I get them free."

"He sells shoe deodorizers—"

"—by the seashore!" She mussed his hair. "We can't all be management consultants!"

Caleb looked down the stairwell and could see hands jerking along the iron banisters. The tramping of feet was a comfortable, human sound.

The bomb threat was the second strange incident at H&L since Caleb had joined the firm. Back in March a cable had snapped on a crane which sat on the roof of a neighboring building. The ton of I-beams which were dangling over the street fell pinwheeling like a fagot of sticks and killed a cabby and his fare. The neck of the crane, long enough to bridge the street, collapsed and, in a sonic boom of an explosion, staved a hole through the side of the Reeves Building and John Beauregard's office, empty, where it pushed over a handsome highboy, decimating the Oriental porcelain on its shelves and flinging books by Peter Drucker and John Kenneth Galbraith across the room. Chunks of plaster and concrete and porcelain covered the maroon carpet. Beauregard's secretary screamed, thinking a bomb had gone off. In the settling dust the iron pulley could be seen sticking through the wall at a slightly upturned angle, an iron trophy head. The secretaries hung up their phones and switched off their typewriters. For a blissful moment the twenty-fifth floor was silent. When Beauregard returned from lunch he was neither surprised nor disturbed; eventually he admitted that the porcelain vases were imitations. On learning that his temporary office would be only three doors down from the Vice Chairman's, he was as pleased as the day he'd bought his home in Greenwich.

After ten flights their legs weakened and, like the others around them, they fell silent. Few voices mixed with the steady tramping. Ahead, a woman in the Technology Group tripped and skinned a knee. As they tired, they found that each flight required more concentration, and navigating twenty simple steps became a challenge—the mind could not keep up.

At last they stepped out onto the hot sidewalk of 47th Street and, walking wobbly-kneed, pushed through the crowd to the curb. They craned their heads for some sign of smoke or destruction.

"Nothing yet," said Grayson.

"Don't hold your breath." It was Diane Landry who spoke. She sat on a fire hydrant. Barefoot, she wiggled her toes.

"You don't think there is a bomb?"

"I doubt there was even a bomb threat. We're witnessing a case of hysteria." She stepped into her shoes.

Grayson said he had heard of the FALN threatening corporations.

"But why us or Langely Insurance or Cuthbert Associates when they have Pan Am, the Helmsley Building,

Colgate-Palmolive over there, and three of the biggest commercial banks and ITT up the street?"

"You've got a point," said Grayson.

"And, assuming there was a bomb, why would the terrorists tell anyone about it? When terrorists bomb buildings it's rarely the architecture they're objecting to."

"Still, just the threat is disruptive," said Grayson.

"But what makes you think it's hysteria?" Caleb asked.

"Some secretary says, 'My mom just called.' The secretary next to her hears something about 'a bomb call,' and the next thing you know there's a bomb scare and the building is evacuated."

"So you think it's our fault," said Jamie.

"Not yours."

"The secretarial staff's."

"Conceivably."

"It may interest you to know that some of us in the general office staff could be on the professional staff if we wanted to be. We have the education. We're not dimwits."

Caleb interrupted. "Grayson and Jamie, you two know Diane Landry, don't you?"

"No relation to the football coach," said Diane. "That's what everyone asks."

"I don't follow football," said Jamie bluntly.

Diane rolled her eyes. "This is getting out of hand. I didn't mean anything against the secretarial staff. I was trying to make the point that this bomb scare is a failure of corporate communications. Don't you see that?"

"Perfectly." Jamie executed an about-face and moved off into the crowd. Grayson shrugged and followed her.

The crowd of Reeves Building employees bulged into the street. Traffic along 47th Street crept by in single file. Hot-dog and ice-cream vendors had discovered the crowd and were wheeling their carts up the sidewalks from Lexington as fast as they could go.

"Want an ice cream, Diane?"

"Nope. Dieting."

"How was your bath?"

"Delicious. How was your birthday?"

"Fine." He didn't volunteer the details.

What to say? What to say? He counted up to the twenty-fifth floor, aware she was watching him.

Word spread among the crowd that the way was clear, the building safe. A string of people started up the block to the Park Avenue entrance, curled around the corner, and seemed to reel the crowd in after them. Caleb walked beside Diane. She mentioned going to see an exhibit at the Guggenheim that night. If he wasn't too busy, he was welcome to join her.

"Do you mean that?"

"Just say yes, Caleb."

"Yes. I'll come."

She had a late meeting to attend so they arranged to meet at the museum.

Caleb's phone was ringing when he returned to his desk.

"Tapolletti here, Sparrow. This is a conference call. I have Walter Jervis, one of our lawyers, on the other line. He's going to explain to you how embarrassing a lawsuit can be to a firm like Hooker & Lyman."

"Mr. Sparrow, Walter Jervis here. Be assured that if you fail to honor the confidentiality of information given to you by Mr. Tapolletti regarding compensation practices at UCI, we will prosecute to the full extent of the law."

Caleb squeezed his eyes shut. "I have assured Mr. Tapolletti, numerous times, of the study's confidential nature. All the salary and bonus figures in the report will be coded. What more does he want?"

"Mr. Sparrow, I think if you recall how many business executives and executive wives have been kidnapped and ransomed over the past few years, you will appreciate Mr. Tapolletti's concern. In almost every case the kidnappings followed disclosures in the press about the executives' income. Mr. Tapolletti is concerned for the safety and well-being of his family."

"He needn't worry."

"Mr. Tapolletti is a cautious man."

There was a lip-smacking noise and breath was exhaled. From the sound of it Mr. Tapolletti was enjoying a cigar while his henchman, Jervis, worked Caleb over.

"But there must be a hundred of these surveys conducted every year. Is this the first he's participated in?"

"I haven't the faintest idea."

"Would you mind asking him?"

Tapolletti's voice, a well of calmness, was right there to answer. "The company has participated in such surveys before, on a limited basis."

"You see, he's just harassing me. And it makes no sense. Do I sound dishonest to you? Do I sound like the sort of person who would do something underhanded?"

"Frankly, Mr. Sparrow, you sound very young."

Tapolletti finally agreed to drop the suit if Caleb would confirm his promise of confidentiality in writing and mail it to UCI within the next two days.

Before leaving for the Guggenheim late that afternoon, Caleb brushed his teeth and combed his hair before the mirror in the men's room. When he emerged he was confronted by Gregory Miller, the Managing Partner, an elegantly dressed man with remarkable poise and self-assurance. Miller shook hands with him and apologized for not introducing himself sooner, a discourtesy he attributed to the reorganization plan he was working on. Very time-consuming. He said he had a minute just then if Caleb wasn't too busy. Flattered Miller even knew his name, Caleb followed him into his office.

The room was identical in size and layout to Beauregard's, but there the similarity ended. In its subdued formality—light-gray walls and beige carpet—and its effort to avoid the charge of pretension, the room had lost whatever style and taste it might have had. Conservative-bland was the closest Caleb could come to describing it. The desk was bare; no sign of a phone.

Miller had been with H&L for fifteen years. He had made a name for himself in the consulting industry by inventing a now widely used method of strategy analysis. Since his appointment as Managing Partner he had devoted himself solely to the day-to-day operations of the firm. Caleb had overheard the secretaries discuss Miller's good looks, and now he saw them for himself. His face had the strong features, rugged masculinity, even the mustache of a Clark Gable, and his gray eyes matched the wallpaper. Caleb had only to exchange a few words with him to confirm that Miller was the quintessential management consultant: smart, polished, attractive.

Caleb was sure that men like Miller didn't have time to spend chatting with subordinates like himself; the Managing Partner was being impressively generous with his time. They talked about the heat wave, college, the value of business school and the MBA. Miller, his chin raised, asked Caleb what he thought of Beauregard and Pike. Caleb answered diplomatically, describing them as intelligent and hard-working. The narrow, straight-backed chair felt like a pew.

"Tough cookies, aren't they?"

"Well, yes, they are." Caleb had heard from Grayson that Miller had once described Pike as prickly. He heard himself use that exact word.

"Pike's got the brains, wouldn't you say?"

"He does. And knows it. He doesn't show Beauregard much respect," said Caleb.

"Why do you suppose that is?"

Caleb attributed it to competitiveness and jealousy. "Not that Pike would like to be Beauregard. He'd like to be a partner."

"Wouldn't you?"

"Of course, sir. In time."

"Are you a Protestant, Caleb?"

"Yes."

"I'm glad for that."

Caleb explained that he wasn't religious, although he had nothing against those who were. His brother was devout; he himself had been confirmed.

"There aren't many of us left," said Miller. "Too many Jews in business."

Caleb, stunned, put his hands on the arms of his chair and started to get up. This was not the kind of discussion he cared to get into.

"You play squash?"

Caleb nodded.

"We'll play soon."

In the hall, head downcast, Caleb went over what had been said. Was that a joke about the Jews? What an extraordinary remark. And he wished now he hadn't answered those questions about Pike and Bureaugard. By passing judgment on them before a superior, he had displayed a deplorable lack of loyalty. He decided that the judicious thing to do would be to play squash with Miller sometime —as painful as that might be—and use the occasion to reaffirm his loyalty to his colleagues and the firm.

9.

Picassos in the Bathroom

CALEB arrived at the Guggenheim before Diane and bought a fudgesicle from a young man with a green Mohawk haircut manning an ice-cream truck. He sat on the low wall with his back to the Rickey and Smith sculptures and the spiraling Frank Lloyd Wright museum, resting his weary legs and happily nibbling his ice-cream bar. Arm in arm, couples passed through the humid evening, and a spectacular raven-haired woman walked a puppy on a leash.

He had to admit that, to date, life had been good to him. His parents had paid for his education and, until his graduation, provided him with an allowance. Except for the occasion during the high-school field trip in New

Haven when a troop of stick-wielding thugs removed his wristwatch, nothing violent had ever happened to him. He had grown up undisturbed on tree-lined streets and broad-lawned campuses, and had always had two or three good male friends. Only recently had he come to realize that, compared to most men his age, he had had few serious relationships; in retrospect, he would have traded some of that ease and comfort for a few more girlfriends.

One question he asked himself was whether a woman would make the difference in his life. By that he meant, would the right woman guarantee his happiness? The thought of a woman doting on him, in and of itself, did not warm his ego. He preferred to think of the right woman as company and no more—forget for a moment the sex and combined incomes. But to get the company you have to have a woman fall in love with you. So whenever he met one he liked, he immediately began to ponder how to make her fall for him, and his thoughts became mathematical. He approached it the way he did his financial analysis. He tried to dream up equations which took into account all her attributes, which were the known variables, and her wants and needs, which were the constants; then he imagined he had only to plug in two or three appropriate endearments and solve for her love.

Nobody had ever explained to him how to go about getting a woman to fall in love. He could impress her with his kindness, but that might be considered calculating; he could be macho, but that was superficial or, worse, threatening. He could act eccentric, but there was nothing alluring about eccentricity—interesting but not romantic. And it didn't help to be smart: that, too, was intimidating.

One old and successful stratagem was to ignore women. Many of them approved of that; of course, then there was the danger he would be ignored in return.

Part of the problem was that he could not interpret a woman's signals. What did it mean if, on a date, she insisted on helping him pay the check? Was she just liberated, or concerned that he could not afford it? Was she afraid that his paying indebted her to him and initiated courtship, a condition she would prefer to avoid, or was she modest, convinced she was undeserving? What about a parting kiss on the cheek rather than on the lips? Did that mean she was chaste, or determined to discourage him at the outset? Always there was ambiguity. He would like nothing better than to ask outright, after the first ten or fifteen minutes, "Well, do you like me or not?" And if she answered affirmatively, have her sign a finely worded contract agreeing to a limited trial relationship.

But tonight would be different. Diane was lively and talkative and he felt no pressure on him to perform. This was the first date in some time which he had actually looked forward to and which he had not approached with the presentiment that dating was work.

Diane was late. He had just licked the last of the ice cream from the stick when he spotted her blue suit a block away. He peered about for a receptacle for the stick and reluctantly flipped it over the wall behind him. As she approached, he felt a stirring inside which he could not quite locate, something akin to a cat's purr. Shaking her hand seemed inappropriate, so he grasped her by the arm, startling her. She stepped back. He said something about the heat and promptly confessed his ice cream.

"Goodness. All this talk all of a sudden. I can see we should get you out more often."

She had brushed a gloss into her hair and put on lipstick. He was virtually certain that she wore the same suit she had worn that morning, and that meant she hadn't been home to change. Had she squeezed in one date already?

"The Guggenheim Museum of Non-Objective Art," she said, looking up at the coils of concrete. "My favorite."

Inside he paid the donations. On the highest ramps overhead only three or four people could be seen moving from painting to painting. Work by Ad Reinhardt, a deceased abstract expressionist, was on display.

"I call him Mad Reinhardt," said Diane. "He doesn't try to justify what he does. You'll see what I mean."

She suggested they start at the bottom and work their way up.

"Walk?" said Caleb. "Up?" He couldn't believe that after twenty-five flights of stairs that afternoon she had the energy to climb the Guggenheim.

"Come, come. We won't go to the top. We'll go as far as the permanent collection. There's a Picasso I want to show you."

They started up the ramp and paused at the first canvas: two black squares overlapped against a black background. In the next canvas, three black squares formed a pyramid. The third was similar, and so was the fourth. All the paintings were black on black.

"This is art for art's sake," said Diane. "Reinhardt said, 'Art is not the spiritual side of business.' I love that. He saw right through the sham of corporate funding of the arts."

"Why are they black?"

"Black is the aggregate of all colors. Too much color and you crowd out light. He's really saying something about light and how it's imperiled by excess. So, in a way, these paintings are about decadence. That's my interpretation. His black paintings make me feel full, as though I've overeaten."

She led him on upward. The muscles in his legs ached. She described Reinhardt's career, his methods of painting, and his place in the New York school of abstract expressionism. She knew exactly which paintings were important and why.

"How do you happen to know so much about him?" Caleb asked, duly impressed.

"When I was at Bennington, I wanted to be a painter. I majored in it. So did my roommate. You couldn't move through our apartment without stepping on canvases and knocking over bottles of brushes. I concentrated on portraits; she painted landscapes—that way we didn't compete. We sat on our stools in our respective corners before our easels and painted stick figures and garish color studies and flat landscapes. I remember we ate a lot of Chinese food because eating with chopsticks made us feel painterly." She smiled as she remembered, her head tipped slightly to one side.

"What made you quit?"

"In February of my senior year I walked into the apartment, took one hard look at my work, acknowledged I had little talent, and enrolled in an accounting course. I did so well the professor encouraged me to apply to business school. The following fall I found myself sitting in an auditorium in Aldrich Hall at Harvard Business School, discussing bankruptcy cases. I had become useful."

A silken strand had worked free of the tortoise-shell comb in her hair, and dangled over her cheek. She smoothed it back into place. They skipped a dozen canvases en route to the permanent collection. She led him to a gray-blue painting of an emaciated woman with elongated arms, ironing.

"Here's one of the most famous paintings from Picasso's Blue Period. When he was in his twenties, he went through a period of personal hardship, and he painted a series of monochromatic paintings, almost all of them blue."

Black, now blue, like my poor feet, thought Caleb.

"My mother once said the painting reminded her of me because the woman in it is skinny and has long arms. That's the influence of El Greco. What I love about the painting is the woman's face—that sad, androgynous pro-file—and the way she's leaning on that iron. Ironing with all her might. It's a painting about monotony."

"She looks ill."

"A spiritual malaise."

Caleb asked her if she missed painting.

"I try not to think about it. It would have taken me fifteen or twenty years to be the kind of painter I wanted to be. Who's got that kind of time? No, I was glad to get over my idealism. It was a handicap. I'll make some money instead, and someday I'll be so rich I'll have Picassos in my bathroom."

She refused to let him walk her home, insisting she had errands to do, although what kind of errands she did at

8 p.m. he couldn't imagine. His legs hurt so badly he didn't complain. They shook hands.

Night to Caleb was just one more Reinhardt canvas stretched across the sky; limping, he paid it little heed in the short painful walk to Yorkville Place.

10.

Fortune-Telling

WEDNESDAY for Caleb was to be a day of number-crunching. He was at his desk by 8:30, fully expecting to spend most of the day there and to see no one except Grayson, Pike, and Diane—if he could think up an excuse to drop in on her. Comfortable in his chair, in high spirits—after all, he had dated the most interesting and attractive woman at H&L—he set to work. Enter first year value, last year value, number of periods; find percent change. Three minutes later Grayson walked in, removed his suit coat, and let snap the latches of his attaché case.

"I don't know about you, Caleb, but after the bomb scare and those damn steps, I was whipped when I got home last night. I was kneeling in front of the tube adjusting the dials. Joan Rivers had just come out on the Carson show.

Suddenly, I got this incredible cramp in my leg and I had to drag myself around the floor trying to find some way to stretch it out, laughing and crying at the same time. Today it's as stiff as a crutch."

Caleb neatly recorded a solution before looking up. "I went to the Guggenheim."

Grayson conceded that, given the limitations of the human body, that was indeed an accomplishment. "With who?"

"Diane Landry."

"Jamie's not big on her." Grayson ducked into his cubicle.

"They hardly know each other," said Caleb.

"You're probably right," came the reply.

"She used to be a painter. Harvard MBA."

Silence, then, "Isn't she a little intense?"

"I like that."

Philip Rasmusen, a reserved Health and Medical researcher, crept in at nine o'clock. He was variously nicknamed "the Crab" and "the Shadow" for his meek, sidewinding shuffle. Grayson had estimated his firm lifespan at six months; Rasmusen had hung on for eight, a phenomenon attributed to bureaucratic oversight and the fact that he had never been reviewed. Grayson maintained that the firm had forgotten he was there.

Leonard Pridgeon appeared ten minutes later holding his sticky, glazed fingers out in front of him and swallowing the last of his Danish while reaching over Caleb's shoulder for a Kleenex.

"Good," he mumbled. A moment later his swivel chair squeaked and shuddered, drawers were rattled open and scraped shut. Pridgeon had begun his belabored morning orientation whispering, "Where was I? Where was I?"

At eleven a.m. Beauregard unexpectedly called a meeting of the Benefact Corp project team. Caleb brought the draft of the report which Linda in Report Production had just returned; he had not had time to proof it. They gathered in the sitting area in Beauregard's office, the partner perched high on his Queen Anne wing chair.

Pike, who was familiar with the data, explained the analysis to Beauregard. They grunted back and forth as they turned the pages. One exhibit wasn't a hundred percent clear to Beauregard, but Pike was sure it could be changed. Caleb nodded confirmation. They agreed the order could be switched. And Pike was going to do the headings himself, if they agreed on the flow and what the data was telling them.

"Benefact has been a good performer since Ransome took charge, wouldn't you agree, Jim?"

"I'd say their major achievement was recapturing some of that lost market share."

"Look here at what the stock's been doing. That's a pretty sight. The shareholders must be pleased."

"Perhaps, but the bottom line is not so good. In fact, if you take out these allowances for discontinued operations, it's a bit shaky; and I don't like the fact that they're so heavily leveraged," said Pike.

"Everyone knew there would be changes when Ransome moved in. I'll venture he's one of the most bold and creative executives out there."

Beauregard had read the same *Wall Street Journal* article Caleb had.

"But, John, some of their return measures are downright mediocre. They paid through the nose for that lost market share. Look at the cost-of-goods-sold and, over here, at the breakdown. And, see, their margins are thin. I think Ransome has gambled he'll get it back next year."

From what Caleb had heard, Pike always led the discussion once the actual presentation began. All Beauregard did was sit back and enjoy his status as the senior guru on strategic planning, toss in a few cogent opinions, and collect the fee when the project was over. He was less interested in the details of the analysis than in what he referred to as "the big picture."

"Jim, I don't know what you're trying to tell me. This company is the darling of the Wall Street press."

"I'm just wondering if we can justify boosting Ransome's salary when the company's a weak performer. Wait until you see the cash flow."

"Is it the man's style you object to? The fact that he fired all those VPs? You forget that a corporation must be commanded."

"John, I'm looking at the facts. I live by facts. I go by what they tell me."

"What does the compensation look like?"

They turned to the compensation section of the report and Caleb's exhibits. Beauregard gave a groan. Not only was Ransome the highest-paid executive in the industry, but his total cash compensation exceeded the amount which Caleb had calculated that he should be making by some $250,000.

"He's at the maximum of his salary range, I take it?" said Beauregard.

"Yes, he's at his max," said Pike. "The guy makes more than Winfield."

Beauregard closed his copy of the report. "The buzz words of executive compensation are: attract, motivate, and retain. Money is what makes the whole system work. I've never met a CEO yet who hasn't gone where the money was. The more they make, the happier they are."

Pike leaned forward in his seat. "But Ransome's pay is a little out of line here, don't you think? It's not as if he could go somewhere else and expect to do as well. Compensation should be an incentive, the carrot on the stick. If it's not, these guys will sit around, do nothing, and wait for their pension to be vested. We've got to link the amount of money they make to the company's performance."

Beauregard looked at the ceiling and ran his tongue over his teeth. "Jim, telling a company how much they should pay their executives is a little like being a daddy and dispensing allowances—too little and the kids are unhappy, too much and they're spoiled."

Pike nodded. "They're spoiling him."

"What do you propose to do?"

"Reduce his salary and increase his bonus potential. Link his bonus to a combination of return on equity and earnings-per-share goals. If he exceeds his goals, he can earn up to a hundred and fifty percent of bonus. If he falls below, then he gets as little as twenty-five percent of bonus. We set tough goals by looking at what the competition is doing. Relative performance. It's a system which works. It provides incentive, believe me. The oil companies have plans like these and so do a handful of other companies. They're just tough enough for the boards to love them. Hewett and TPF&C are making a fortune selling them."

Beauregard seemed not to have heard. Finally he said, "Jim, I'm not knocking the plan—it's a good one—but this presentation is to the Executive Committee and not the full Board. These are the guys who hired Ransome. They may be worried about losing him. If not to a competitor, to the government. Reagan considered him a top prospect for his cabinet."

"Let me run with this, John. I can have some exhibits slapped together which will knock their socks off."

"What are we getting for this study?"

"Eighty thousand."

"Tops?"

"Tops."

"This is a prestige client. Be a shame to lose it."

"I won't lose it."

Beauregard looked at his watch, a thin gold Piaget his wife had given him on his fiftieth birthday. The inscription, which he had proudly shown Caleb, read: "For J.B., from Dee-Dee." Beauregard was crazy about his wife and had once remarked, "If there were a Fortune 500 of wives, she would be on it."

"Today is Wednesday. That gives us a week until the meeting—not a lot of time. I'll be in Cleveland through next Monday, so you're on your own. But don't overlook the nutritive aspects of compensation. And, Caleb, do me a favor—get your hair cut. These are important people and I don't want you looking like a bum."

* * *

Caleb knocked and poked his head into Diane's office. "With you in a minute," she said without looking up.

She could work the keys of her calculator with the fingers of her left hand, simultaneously recording numbers with her right—a technique taught at the Big Eight accounting firms, where calculator proficiency was a celebrated means to increased productivity. Caleb had heard of one firm which sponsored an annual world series of button-punching and another which offered a lucrative fellowship to dexterous college seniors. He wondered where she had learned the method.

Pike didn't think she was a typical Harvard MBA: "Not arrogant enough." He had interviewed her a year ago when she was first applying to H&L. His interview assignment had been to assess her quantitative ability; someone else measured her overall business savvy, and a third judged her interpersonal skills. She had baffled them all by drawing farfetched analogies between wampum and generally accepted accounting principles, and by simply refusing to answer questions she considered personal. Her grades and her recommendations were superb. Furthermore, as Beauregard had remarked, "Once you got talking to her, you almost forgot she was a woman." All qualms the firm had about hiring her vanished when it was learned that Booz, Allen & Hamilton had extended her an exploding offer: a bonus of $1,000 if she accepted their job within a week. Miller matched Booz, Allen's offer and threw in free dental insurance.

She spoke her mind in client meetings; she corrected grammar ("impact is not a verb"); she successfully petitioned to have the ladies' room enlarged; and in her annual appraisal she earned an A rating. The only thing she didn't do was take a boyfriend. Reports came in from the few men who dated her that she was frigid or a lesbian, the kind of misinformation designed to hide hurt feelings and disappointment, and not without effect: almost overnight the men in the office stopped asking her out.

Pike had the following explanation for her professional success. "Her work is not her life and, because it's not, the stakes for her aren't as high. She has no fear of failure and thus can take chances in what she says and does. Therefore her work is brilliant; her ascent could be meteoric. But the thing to remember is that her commitment is limited."

Pike said Miller had plans to marry her off to a top client.

When she looked up, Caleb could detect some weariness, and yet her eyes glowed.

"Free for lunch?"

"You couldn't have picked a worse day to ask me. To-morrow is completely ruined by that seminar, and I'm behind as it is."

"Seminar?"

"Oh, Caleb, how could you forget the renowned Dr. Fine and his team dynamics?"

She laughed a sleigh-bell laugh and made him grin despite the buck of panic.

Back at his desk Caleb asked Grayson if he knew that the all-firm seminar was the next day. Grayson nodded.

"Oh, shit!" said Pridgeon from his corner.

"And we have a meeting for all the researchers at five today," said Grayson.

"What!" said Caleb.

"Didn't you get a memo on that?"

"I guess I must have."

"Remember, it said cocktails would be served."

"They sent that out weeks ago."

"And you're supposed to remember."

Caleb threw up his arms. "You know, I feel like I'm playing at working and that I'm not accomplishing anything. It must be because I have so much work to do."

Grayson suggested they take a lunch break. He was working on a project for the Commissioner of the U.S. Football League, attempting through survey and analysis to determine what net effect rule changes such as abolishing facemasks would have on attendance. The deadline was not for another three weeks.

On the way to Ned's Burger Cottage at 45th and Lexington, Caleb asked Grayson a question he had been meaning to ask him for some time.

"What happens if, after business school, you discover you don't want to spend your whole life in business? I mean, how can you honestly be so sure business is what you should be doing? Doesn't it scare you that you may live here and do pretty much what we do today until the day you retire, and the only difference will be you eat in better restaurants?"

An indefatigable worker and adroit corporate technician, Grayson studied each assignment at the outset and negotiated for the work he could handle and excel at. When a problem arose, he would burrow among the data to solve it, the paper and transfiles mounting around him. As a last resort, he would approach Pike or another principal, steer him out of the hall toward his desk, his questions couched in flattery. He knocked on every door before entering, chuckled his low, staccato chuckle at all the jokes, and worked long hours. He had put himself through college and had every intention of going much further. He once showed Caleb a folder full of his business school acceptances.

"I don't let myself ask those questions. If I stopped to think why I'm doing what I'm doing, somebody might notice and question my commitment. Then I'd be looked over for a promotion or pushed off the fast track. I'm going to the top, Caleb, and I'm not looking back until I get there. You should do the same. Your kind of thinking can hurt you in business, especially at H&L. When we're CEOs someday and going to Hawaii on business trips and we have what they call 'fuck-you money,' you'll agree that all the nonsense we put up with was worth it."

"But are you sure you'll feel you've done something worthwhile?"

"There aren't many things in life that *are* worthwhile. At least doing this you can have a family and live comfortably—which I happen to think is worthwhile. Who do you know who really expects to change the world? I mean, these are the eighties. It's too late to change things. At least in business you have an environment that can maintain itself. It's not perfect, but it works, it balances. Records are kept and you can understand what's happening and why. I like that about it. I like that a lot. And, Caleb, did it ever occur to you that somebody must take responsibility for our institutions? They're not going to run themselves."

Some people, like Grayson, could bring out the best in their friends, could inspire them—they were natural role models, even without being saints. The reaction they provoked was: I admire and respect this person; I want him to admire and respect me. From then on everyone was on his best behavior. Caleb hoped to develop that capacity. The secret to being a role model and a leader, he perceived, was to know who you were and what you wanted out of life. To achieve that would take some doing.

Grayson and Caleb passed a construction site where workers sat side by side eating lunch on a stack of wood chosen for its view of the street and the passing pedestrians.

"Those poor bastards. What a life," said Grayson.

Caleb said nothing; he had just been thinking how cozy they looked.

At Ned's, Grayson ate with the same determination with which he performed his duties at H&L. He devoured his burger in a single bout of chewing. Caleb, on first witnessing this display, had stared and let his own burger cool. Grayson had cleaned his plate, wiped his mouth and fingers with a napkin, and covered his check with a five-dollar bill before Caleb so much as took a bite.

"No wonder you get indigestion," he said.

"I'm conditioning my stomach to work fast. I figure I can add half an hour to the day."

Bob Sparrow's secretary, Wendy, telephoned that afternoon to say Caleb's father had four tickets to a fight at Madison Square Garden Friday night and would Caleb like to come and bring along two friends.

Caleb called over to Grayson, "Any interest in seeing a fight on Friday? My old man's got tickets."

Grayson leaned out into the aisle. "Boxing? Why not?"

"My stepmother is in Switzerland visiting relatives and when she's away the old man doesn't know what to do with himself. He's going to take us out for dinner beforehand."

"Sounds great."

"I'll invite Dale, my roommate. I owe him one."

Gregory Miller, Managing Partner, Tony Graves, Director of Personnel, and Bronson Normby, Director of Professional Development, sponsored an informal cocktail party for the research analysts at five p.m. as planned. The gathering was to celebrate the fifth anniversary of the research program and to foster camaraderie among its members.

Caleb had spoken to Tony Graves once or twice in the halls since his initial interview. Graves called him "sport"; evidently he had forgotten Caleb's name. Bronson Normby had been at charm school. The onetime senior partner had been a victim of a famous interfirm reorganization shortly after Miller was named Managing Partner. His so-called "lateral transfer" was nothing more than a demotion. Normby, a fidgety man passionately loyal to the firm, had authored its official history. Caleb remembered him saying that Mr. Hooker had walked three miles to work each morning and two more home each night (Caleb assumed he took a shortcut) and that Mr. Lyman—stone deaf— had lip-read and loved cats.

The three H&L executives were standing at a bar in the

twenty-sixth-floor conference room soberly talking among themselves when Grayson, Leonard Pridgeon, Philip Rasmusen, and Caleb arrived in a group.

"Here comes the future of this firm," said Miller, raising his glass to toast them.

"Here, here," said Normby heartily.

Graves smiled in silence.

Grayson shook each man's hand, and Caleb and the others followed his example. The four twenty-sixth-floor researchers arrived: quadruplets in blue. After another round of handshaking the researchers helped themselves to drinks. Caleb opened a Heineken; Grayson poured himself a drink to be sociable, but never took a sip.

During an average day the twenty-fifth-floor researchers saw little of their twenty-sixth-floor counterparts. They were eager to learn if their work was the same, their hours as long, if anyone was in danger of being fired. The researchers stood in a group on one side of the room, the older executives on the other. Caleb talked to Mike Stevens, the researcher assigned to the Allied project. Stevens had spent the last nine months running numbers for the project, but he had flown to Dallas twice to collect data and spent a week with his team on a working retreat in the Caribbean.

"The firm paid for that?"

"We were under budget. We billed it to the client."

"How do you get away with that?"

"Oh, no, Caleb. The client expects it."

Normby had three cocktails in the first fifteen minutes. When Caleb spoke to him, Normby kept repeating how impressed he was with the research personnel. His eyes brimmed with good-will tears.

Miller clinked his glass with a fountain pen. "As you know, this day marks the fifth anniversary of the research program. A program that I initiated and, therefore, one I feel especially close to.

"I decided the time had come to do an evaluation, and so I made an effort over the past week to speak to each of you individually. My findings have been most encouraging. I can say unequivocally that the program is now a success and that the research analysts at H&L are here to stay."

Normby clapped and the researchers politely contributed.

"The credit for this program belongs to Tony Graves, who recruited you, and to you yourselves, who have proved so deserving of our confidence. Now, I don't want to take much more of your time with a speech—we're here to enjoy a quiet little celebration—but I do want to show you that the firm is prepared to put its money where its mouth is. This morning I ordered computer terminals to be installed at each of your desks. This is our way of thanking you. Furthermore, for those of you who are unfamiliar with the operations and applications of this extraordinary tool, the firm is going to send you to night school, tuition-free."

White flashed from a photographer's strobe: the announcement would be in the H&L newsletter.

Night school! thought Caleb, his belly clenching. When would he find the time to go to night school?

11.

The Flock

HAIRCUTS were cheap at the Blue Ribbon Barber Shop. The barbers trimmed and shaved a steady flow of customers, most of them gray-haired and sixtyish, members of the subway crowd at 86th Street. Caleb didn't mind that there was no stylist or manicurist, or no blow dryers and warming lights; he didn't mind vinyl-covered chairs with chrome arms or the tickling odor of ammonia which met him when he reached over to retrieve a *Sports Illustrated* from the floor. He wanted a practical, no-frills trim, Beauregard's orders; he wanted to ensure he looked neat for the presentation—to say nothing of Diane and any women he might meet at Ruth Ross's cocktail party later this evening.

Between haircuts the Blue Ribbon barbers washed

meticulously, soaping their hands in a sink against the far wall, then rinsing, palms up with a panning-for-gold motion.

Vinny, the oldest, waved Caleb to his chair. Vinny had a head like a cantaloupe, bald except for a gray monkish fringe. He could cut three heads of hair in the time it took his colleagues to cut two. He began on one side of the chair and snipped his way around to the other side, then trimmed with an electric trimmer, vacuumed, and wet-combed. Revisions were rare. The other barbers would whisk the sheet off with a flourish of a painter unveiling a portrait, but Vinny slid it off smoothly and shook it, a matador luring a bull.

Caleb was pumped to the desired height. He glanced once at his features in the mirror and concluded that he looked mournful when he should be happy. It was that genetic Sparrow look.

Vinny worked slower today than usual. At last he held up a hand mirror, providing Caleb with a rare rear view. The trim was not what he had wanted: too short, a marine cut in back, half-moons over each ear. Suppressing a pang of disappointment, he thanked Vinny and tipped high.

Ruth Ross, formerly Annette Funkhauser, had changed her name while at Denison when she took up drama. She had played Nora in *A Doll's House*, her one lead role, in a show she had also directed. Her voice, Caleb recalled, had projected with admirable clarity, but her body was at odds with the confines of the stage. She tripped on props and sideswiped other members of the cast. Nevertheless, she felt predestined to storm Broadway or to program-exec successful sit-coms for ABC. In the two years since she graduated, she had helped backstage on a few showcases. Recently she had taken to giving large, expensive parties to widen her field of acquaintances and to help promote her career. This would be her third party in a year and the second to which Caleb had been invited.

Caleb arrived at the RCA Building midtown, feeling prosperous and respectable in a freshly dry-cleaned tan two-piece suit. He followed signs to the Rainbow Room and, humming, rode the elevator to the floor below the famous ballroom, where rooms could be rented for private parties.

A tidy, petite woman he didn't recognize sat at a card table, a cashbox open before her. She asked for ten dollars as a donation. He was sure there had been no mention of a cover charge on the invitation. Before paying, he counted his bills, thinking that he should have brought more. She stamped the back of his hand with a red dollar sign.

Ruth Ross, her neck wrapped in a black feather boa, greeted her guests in the alcove beside the coat room. Four or five of her male entourage, conspicuous in black tie, grim as bodyguards, stood near her at all times. Ruth used them to create a diversion if she failed to match a name to an approaching face.

She kissed Caleb, dry pecks on both cheeks. To those who kept track of such things, the progression from a handshake to a Ruth Ross kiss was a social promotion; she reserved her kisses for those she deemed most likely to succeed.

Noticing his hair, she rocked back to get a better look

and crooned, "What a hairdo! Why, you look fourteen years old. What did that cost you?"

Caleb ran his hands over his scalp. "It only looks that way because it's just been cut."

"You should tell me who did it so I can warn people, or beautiful men will be hurt."

"It's just a haircut."

"Some haircut. Jill Shephard, do you know Caleb Sparrow? Look what a barber did to his hair. I've seen better-looking wall-to-wall carpeting."

Jill Shephard, a tanned beauty, thick hanks of auburn hair cascading over her shoulders, was paying little attention. She looked at Caleb for a moment. She reminded him of a woman in a Third Avenue bar who some months before, when he had tried to engage her in conversation, had advised him to "stick it." That had been one of those moments when he wondered if he was emotionally fit to deal with New York women.

"What do you do, Caleb?"

"Consulting."

"You and everyone else." She sashayed off toward a group of men, a peacock with her feathers spread.

"By the way, Caleb—" Ruth's hand with its ruby nails lay on his arm—"Your old flame Amy Hoagland is here somewhere and asked after you."

"Thanks. I'll see if I can find her."

He looked over the crowd and recognized Bill Addison, an associate at Morgan Stanley, and Addison's roommate, Burt Trelawney, a Time Incer, drinks in their fists, looking as groomed as retrievers at a dog show. They were not, he noticed, in the company of any of the young actresses or cover girls they usually brought to parties. Caleb could see Gil Philips at the bar, a Baker Scholar from the Harvard Business School, now at Goldman Sachs and only twenty-two years old; Hugh Hutchinson, a nationally ranked squash-player while in college and now a trainee at E. F. Hutton; George Shea, a research analyst at McKinnsy; Oliver Hartsdale, an accountant at Coopers & Lybrand credited with working New York's longest documented work week: 147 hours.

The crowd included one or two oddballs—gate-crashers or friends of invited guests—among them Owen Bickle, who discussed sex with unsettling candor, recommending positions and fetishes the way most people recommend books or movies. ("Stepladder: greatest invention since the waterbed.") Other outsiders included Roland Wakefield from Greenwich, Connecticut, who had never done anything and possessed what he referred to, frequently, as a "cushion," and Mary Variwell, Ruth's rival who was rarely seen outside Doubles. When Mary's agent failed to get her the cover of *Town & Country*, she surprised the Doubles crowd by appearing instead in the pages of *Playboy*, where, according to an impressed Owen Bickle, she proved to be something of a contortionist. She was on the arm of a German prince whose lengthy name Caleb could never remember.

Those were the exceptions Caleb spotted right away, and they weren't numerous. This was a successful and sophisticated group: a herd of proud and elegant corporate aspirants, their hair parted and combed, their suits well tailored, their shoes shined. He was confident that one day they would manage the banks, corporations, law firms of New York, and shoulder the responsibility for progress. They would occupy the corner offices and own the view. They would find their pots of gold. And if they must wait a few more years for all this, they could, on occasion, rent the space.

"They say he's a prodigy, and if he can keep his nose clean, he'll be a VP in two years."

"I love Sotheby's, but I couldn't work there if Daddy didn't pay my rent."

Caleb bought a bourbon and ginger.

From the windows of the Rainbow Room, Manhattan's rulered streets could be seen, lined with the world's best companies, stores, hotels, restaurants, and night clubs— streets lit with gold ascending into a pitch-black sky. The Promised Land.

Caleb could imagine what it must be like to be the head of a corporation, to confer with the Board and deliver finely tuned decisions which would trim, tighten, and spur the organization, which would inspire the staff. He could envision orchestrating a galaxy of people and products, ensuring they remained neatly ordered and governed by the friendly and familiar laws, not of mass and gravity, but of supply and demand. He felt worthy, well apprenticed, ready, when who should walk across his line of vision but Dale, the Chap Stick junky. Caleb drew a long breath as he realized that the only way Dale could have known about this party was by reading his mail.

At the bar he ordered a second drink.

"Someone has to die or give birth for there to be a promotion in publishing."

"He made his fortune selling pork bellies."

"The case method is under fire. Even Bok of Harvard has criticized it. You're better off going to Stanford."

"He earned twenty thousand dollars in residuals for a five-second spot."

Amy Hoagland found him. Her face now, although still pretty, was round, not oval, and her arms looked swollen. He had not spoken to her in a year: since their commencement, when he shook hands with her parents and her grandparents simply to be polite, and the grandmother kept asking, "Are you the young man? Are you the young man?" And Amy, blushing, quietly explained that no, this was not the young man. Then he had seen her once ahead of him, pushing through a turnstile at the 59th Street stop of the IRT, and he had remained on the platform studying a movie poster of a young garroted beauty until she was out of sight.

"Pristine."

"Pristine?"

"My new account. A deodorant for the working woman. We roll out the fall campaign this week with a spot-ad budget of one-point-two million, which, if successful, will make Pristine a household word like Ms. or Maxi Pad. Can you imagine time better spent?" Talking to Amy reminded Caleb of the junior lifesaving exam where you had to swim dragging a limp body back and forth the length of the pool.

"Why so sarcastic?"

"I hate it."

"What you're doing is marketing, which is business."

"You expect me to take the advertising racket seriously?"

"What about the money?"

"The money is okay."

"Well, there you go."

"You call that a case for working in advertising? Is everything so black and white to you? You used to be so idealistic. Don't you have any causes?"

"Causes for worry."

"Oh, come on! What have you got to worry about?"

They stood in silence and sipped their drinks, Amy piqued, Caleb contemplative. Recently, on a crowded elevator, a woman with a punk haircut and one made-up eye had caught him smiling to himself over a joke he had heard at lunch. She'd whispered to him, "I bet you work for a bank and love your job. You suits gross me out!" He'd wanted to make some clever retort, but the elevator door had opened and she'd stepped off.

"How's life otherwise?" Caleb asked, seeking to make amends.

"Oh, it's the life of your average working girl. A month ago my apartment was burglarized. Now they're fixing a water main in my building and I've been without running water for three days. Yesterday I had to cancel my Club Med vacation because it coincides with an important AIA meeting. Do you think Mary Wells Lawrence had to put up with this? Otherwise life is wonderful. Every man I meet is either ancient or gay. How are Will and Henry?"

Will Rollings and Henry Barrett had been Caleb's roommates as well as his two best friends at Denison.

"Will is getting a PhD in economics at the University of Texas. Henry went abroad to travel, hoping to postpone

127

his entry into the corporate world. He ended up broke in Geneva and accepted a job with a chocolate company. I haven't talked to either of them in months."

"I'm surprised. You guys were close."

Amy used to sit with them when they drank and smoked until dawn, hatching fanciful get-rich-quick schemes or talking about who in history they would most like to have been—Will saw himself as Karl Marx, Henry wanted to be Charles Darwin, Caleb wished he had been Socrates, and Amy admired Cleopatra. All that seemed long ago.

"They're busy. *I'm* busy. Besides, in a few years' time they'll end up in New York. Everyone does."

"Probably love it here, too. Like you." She punched his arm. "Sorry. Guess I shouldn't be so negative. My mother's always getting on me for my bad attitude."

The hors d'oeuvres, pellets of pastry stuffed with cheese, were served on a bed of wilted lettuce. Caleb took one, chewed tentatively, swallowed. Nearby, Jill Shephard linked arms with her date. His name was Martin Sorenson and he modeled suits for Ralph Lauren, smoked cigarettes for Kool, and drank beer for Michelob. His green crushed-velvet tuxedo, he explained, was by Bill Blass—$340—his slippers by Bally—$310.

"I could have been a lawyer," he told his audience. "But why not do something you enjoy and live a little?" He scooped a handful of hors d'oeuvres off the passing tray and popped them in his mouth. He chewed open-mouthed with juicy diction.

Jill elaborated on his career, listing the commercials and the publications he had appeared in, how his agent described him as a switchblade-wielding version of Michelangelo's *David*. She announced that Martin had made $100,000 last year and that they were going to Nice in August to celebrate.

"Which is not to say it's easy to be a model, male or female," said Martin. "You have to act in order to show the kind of emotion a situation requires. For example, you might have to take a bite out of a cheeseburger, and, to do it right, you have to first convince yourself that it's the best damn cheeseburger you've ever tasted and then take your bite. You might have to take twenty or thirty bites of hamburger, convincing yourself each time that the next bite is going to be the greatest. Modeling demands skill and mental discipline."

"Tell them about the beer commercial."

"I did one beer commercial in which I drove a road-grater. A good role, but they couldn't use my hands in the scene where we sit around afterwards and have a beer. I once broke two fingers in a touch football game and they didn't heal straight. Do you believe that the guy who played my hands made more money for that commercial than I did? That gives you an idea of how competitive the business is. It's not enough to have a pretty face."

Jill caressed the side of his head and snagged her fingers in his curls.

Alfred Parrish, Webster '80, economics major, Olympus Brands training program, tapped Caleb on the shoulder. "Can I talk to you for a second?"

Caleb walked with him to the window, where Parrish stood looking at the street below.

"They let me go last week," he said.

"I don't believe it."

Parrish had been one of those at Denison who lined up outside the career-services office at 6:30 a.m. in subzero weather to be sure he was granted an interview with every company recruiting at the college.

"I made some mistakes, I know I did. But they never let me get my feet on solid ground."

"Anything I can do?" asked Caleb, thinking he should get Parrish away from the window. "I could call my old man." He wished he hadn't said it.

"Call your old man? Not only has he never heard of me, I doubt he's ever heard of my Division."

"What are you going to do?"

"I'm going to apply for a job at my old high school, teaching math, relax a bit."

"Well, sure. Nothing wrong with that."

"Glad I have your approval."

Parrish wanted to be sure Caleb didn't forget to throw out his business card. "If you want to get in touch with me, call my folks in Passaic."

At the bar, buying a drink for Amy, Caleb spoke with the Morgan Stanley associate, Bill Addison.

"I understand you landed a job at H&L," said Addison.

"Yes."

"What do you know? When I heard what a hotshot your old man is, I asked myself why does Caleb bother to work at all? H&L. Got to hand it to you. From there it's on to Harvard Business School."

"We'll see." How odd to be commended for bothering to work. People should know him better than that. Caleb could not take seriously the possibility he might one day inherit some money. His father was fifty-two and, if his grandfather's longevity was any indication, would live to be ninety. That would make Caleb nearly the age of retirement before he received his inheritance, assuming there was something left to inherit.

What annoyed Caleb more than the issue of money was that people seemed to think that wealth made his father a great man. Now, not everyone can make money, and he wasn't about to denounce his father as a less than great man, but what did money have to do with greatness? My God, thought Caleb, I must be a Marxist. And then he remembered Amy's remark about money, with its presumption that he had changed and not, as Pike would say, for the better. Didn't she see what was happening—and not just to him but to all the men and women entering the job market? They had emerged from college thinking the world was new, fresh from the wrapper and waiting to be devoured, only to discover that the companies and institutions of the country were overcrowded and largely indifferent to their arrival. Security, the search for it, ballooned in importance.

Addison, a drink clamped in his hand, wished Caleb luck.

"Bill, what do you know about Jack Ransome of Benefact Corp? He has retained us to do some compensation work."

To ask such a question was a breach of professional conduct—H&L forbade members of the firm to discuss projects with outsiders, or in any way to reveal their client or the nature of the assignment. But Addison would have an informed opinion on Ransome—Morgan Stanley was Benefact Corp's investment banker. And if he was impressed with Caleb's proximity to the corporate greats, well, that didn't hurt Caleb or H&L.

"Pistol-bearing Jack Ransome. A maverick, always a one-man show. Love him or leave him. I would never work for him."

Caleb said he needed to get some sleep.

"Sleep-sheep. That's all you do is sleep. We're going to have a nightcap," Dale, arm around Caleb's shoulders, enunciated in his ear—"or two."

Caleb had long since forgiven Dale for reading his mail and crashing the party. Late at night in New York there were advantages to having a roommate.

In the glowing street light the sidewalks glittered with stars of mica. The heat and humidity had abated and the air held instead the coolness of a Canadian jack-pine forest. Overhead rose the Chrysler Building, with scalloping and motorcar gargoyles, its needle pointing into the sky. Walter P. Chrysler. How lucky one would have to be to achieve a fraction of that success! And yet on such a night success seemed not only possible but imminent.

Dale and Caleb stood on the sidewalk debating where to go.

"BBQs—Brooklyn, Bronx, or Queens," murmured Dale, noting the approach of two young women wearing tight jeans and flouncy, diaphanous blouses. He addressed the taller of the two, the one who returned his stare, asked if he knew her from somewhere. She shrugged. Dale said he wished he did, at which point she looked at her friend and gave a wry smile.

"Sure you do."

"Let me prove it." Dale made the introductions. "I'm Gary, this is John. We'll buy you a drink."

"Ellen. She's Beth."

"My name is not John," said Caleb thickly.

The two women giggled in harmony; smiles gouged their cheeks.

"Use it," said Dale in a low voice, stepping off the curb to flag a cab.

"What do you do?" the little one, Beth, asked.

"I'm an ornithologist."

"Is that like a chiropractor?"

"Not much." He whistled his best birdsong, the clear, looping call of the Baltimore oriole, then, lifting his chin and closing his eyes—the black behind his lids had a coarse grain—the machine-gun whistle of the field sparrow. No signs of comprehension. The woman named Ellen seemed to be trying to read his wristwatch. Arms akimbo, he gave what he assured them would be an easy one to recognize: quail. The three notes had the requisite clarity, but the timing was bad, rushed.

"We better find him a cage!" said Beth in a breathy whisper.

All four climbed into the back of the Checker, Beth grabbing him by the wrist and pulling him in beside her. She squirmed and rearranged herself so she sat snug in his lap. The cab started with a jerk. She wore the spicy, incense-oil perfume which had been popular in the sixties. The concavity of her cheeks and the flat blackness of her hair suggested American Indian, but her complexion, its pale tone, gave her the ethnic stamp of an Italian. She ran her hard fingers over his chest and kissed his lips.

Caleb had encountered three distinct varieties of kissers: those whose dry, rubbery-lipped kiss was hard to pardon, those whose kiss was as soft and wet as a bite of ripe peach, and those whose kiss wrapped around the mouth like a gag, ground teeth against teeth, and sucked the breath away. Beth, although light and cuddly in his lap, was of the third variety, and Caleb was struggling for air before it was over. He grinned, blushed in the dark. He had almost forgotten what it was like to hold a woman in his arms— the sensual fairgrounds of necking. Someone must have put in a good word for him with the wish-granter. To his right Dale and Ellen grappled and slid half onto the floor. The girls must be airline stewardesses, thought Caleb, a thought interrupted by a second submersion. Why did it seem so natural to kiss an absolute stranger? Although these were, at moments, carnal, hungry kisses, they seemed primarily youthful and mischievous, like kissing a first cousin. Caleb promised to remind himself to party more; he had been missing out on life's more adventuresome aspects.

The cab stopped for a light on 79th Street. Ellen sat bolt upright.

"Beth, we got to go!"

"I thought we were going drinking," said Dale.

"Do you see what time it is? My old man's going to kill me." She told the cabby to pull over.

"Your old man? You mean your dad? How old are you?"

"Seventeen."

"Holy, holy," said Dale.

At the curb Beth and Ellen climbed out. They stood on the sidewalk and blew kisses. Beth crossed her arms and shivered; Caleb waved to her. The slammed door chopped her off from Caleb's view.

"What teamwork. We ought to go out together more often." Dale sat with his knees wide apart. Out came the Chap Stick. "That doesn't happen very often, not even to me. Driver, better make that Ninety-first and Third."

When the cab pulled up in front of Yorkville Place, Dale insisted on paying, but, reaching for his wallet, he froze, puzzled, then astonished, and moaned—as Caleb groped hopelessly for his—"Why, those little tramps!"

Caleb, birding, had at first assumed that the species which passed through Westchester County during migration traveled like geese in orderly flocks. Later he had sighted numerous birds flying alone at night, feeding during the day. Only the lucky ones flew in flocks, and he had read a violent loneliness into this discovery. It was additional evidence that life had a mean streak.

Back in their apartment Dale rummaged through the kitchen cupboards in search of something to drink. He found a bottle of green crème de menthe, origin unknown, and this he and Caleb drank on the rocks, lamenting their misfortune and the cruel ways of the city. They toasted the pickpockets for their cunning and the cab-driver for accepting a personal check. Caleb, in bed at last, slept fitfully.

12.

The Case Method

I n a small, crowded amphitheater a group of students sat facing a wall of blackboards. On each desk stood a cardboard placard with the student's name inscribed in red Magic Marker letters. The class was discussing Caleb's case.

The professor, who bore an uncanny resemblance to Bob Sparrow, called on Martin Sorenson.

Martin: "I don't understand why Caleb doesn't have a girl. Looks aren't everything, and he strikes me as a normal sort of person. Is it that he's so uptight?"

Mary Variwell: "If Caleb were to come up to me in Doubles, I'd buy him a drink."

Jill Shephard: "I bet you would! Frankly, if I were his

supervisor at H&L, I would terminate him. He thinks too much."

Professor: "Let's have a show of hands who would fire Caleb Sparrow. . . . Roughly two-thirds. Mr. Addison, what's your opinion?"

Bill Addison: "I ask myself who is to blame? Isn't that the gist of this case? Do you blame his parents for not loving him enough? For getting divorced? For spoiling him? Or is it his own fault? His old man is some kind of guy. Too bad more of that entrepreneurial drive didn't rub off on Caleb."

Professor: "Mr. Parrish, how do you respond to that?"

Alfred Parrish: "I haven't prepared the case, sir."

Professor: "Do you intend to loop Business Policy?"

Alfred Parrish: "No, sir. I was up all night preparing for Human Resource Management."

Professor: "Perhaps the next case you should prepare, Mr. Parrish, is your suitcase. Mr. Ault, if you were Caleb, what would you do?"

Grayson: "First I would get on the computer and write a program for multi-variable regressions. Then I would enter the data and determine the correlation coefficient of relatedness. If I got a good correlation—of, say, .8 or better—I would feel comfortable projecting a meaningful solution."

Professor: "And if the correlation was low?"

Grayson: "I'd average."

Professor: "Doesn't that analysis strike any of you as a bit clinical? Is anyone uncomfortable with that procedure? . . . Mr. Bickle?"

Owen Bickle: "A computer can't take into consideration our emotions and our drives. I mean, Caleb could be horny. That would explain a lot."

Professor: "Mr. Abernathy?"

Dale: "Me? I guess I'd wing it. You know, guesstimate."

Professor: "You feel comfortable doing that?"

Dale: "I realize it's not scientific or professional or whatever, but I feel okay doing it."

Professor: "What about the haircut? Would you have had your hair cut if you were Caleb?"

Dale: "Too risky. Barbers are unreliable people. You tell them what you want—just over the ears, a little off the top, don't touch the sideburns—and then they go ahead and do what they feel like."

Grayson: "It was sheer vanity on Caleb's part, and bound to get him in trouble. He just doesn't know how to take advice."

Ruth Ross: "He's cheap."

Amy Hoagland: "I have to agree with Grayson. Caleb has poor judgment. And this is just one example. Going back to the girlfriend business, you should see the kind of women he has been dating."

Professor: "Mr. Addison, did you calculate the probability of Caleb making CEO at H&L?"

Bill Addison: "I did. I came up with one in a thousand."

Professor: "That seems a little low. Ms. Shephard?"

Jill Shephard: "One in twenty thousand. He just doesn't have the stuff."

Professor: "Any others?"

Owen Bickle: "I'd sooner bet on the lottery."

Professor: "Let's call it one in twenty thousand. Anyone think to ask Caleb's brother, Robert, what he thought of Caleb's career choice?"

Grayson: "I tried, but he doesn't have a phone. His church doesn't believe in telecommunications."

Professor: "Any questions?"

Ruth Ross: "It's not really a question. I went out with a guy like this once. He wrote charming letters, very affectionate, but when I was actually with him he was a cold fish. Never showed emotion. I count my blessings I'm not married to someone like that."

Martin Sorenson: "What if he had his teeth straightened?"

Owen Bickle: "Maybe if he masturbated . . ."

Amy: "He told me birds were evidence of God's grace, but I heard he once shot an albatross."

Jill Shephard: "I believe it."

Dale: "Caleb told me that what he really wanted in life was a Ferrari."

Bill Addison: "With automatic transmission."

Professor: "It may interest you to know that H&L did not fire Caleb Sparrow. But nor did he have a celebrated career. He led a normal life. Although he never made partner, he provided well for his wife and four sons. Today he is approaching the age of mandatory retirement and talks often about returning to his high school to teach math. His youngest son recently scored eight hundred on the GMAT and appears destined for business school."

13.

TEST

Every two months H&L sponsored an all-day seminar for its professional staff. Although the topics varied—"Graphic Display of Financial Data: Some New Ideas"; "Planting the Decision Tree"; "A Stylistic Approach to Public Speaking" were three Caleb had attended —the setting was always a Waldorf-Astoria ballroom transformed into a classroom. The H&L professionals sat at long parallel rows of tables under crystal chandeliers.

Caleb slid his briefcase onto one of these tables and sat down opposite Diane.

"What's the tape for?" she asked, running her thumb along a peeling strip of masking tape.

"That covers my grandfather's monogram. I don't want people to think I stole the briefcase."

"Aren't you just making it more conspicuous by trying to hide it?"

"His name was Christian Inch Aldrich. People were bugging me on the subway."

"That's different."

"My maternal grandfather, an insurance salesman. My mother gave me the briefcase along with his cufflinks when I graduated from college."

"A briefcase is a wonderful thing, don't you think? I find it heartening to know that the work of one's life can be made compact and portable."

"Room here?" asked Pike, drawing out the chair beside Diane.

"That's mine," said Diane, removing the pocketbook that lay on it.

"Jim, you remember Diane Landry."

"Sure. You're the one who's no relation to the football coach."

"None whatsoever."

Pike shook off his jacket and hooked it over the back of his chair. He sat down, tightened his necktie knot, and stretched his feet, bumping Caleb's.

"Are those things tough to clean?" he asked Diane, pointing to the chandeliers.

"What makes you think I clean chandeliers?"

"Intuition," said Pike, still gazing skyward.

Caleb spotted Grayson at the far end of the room and waved to him. Grayson joined them; seated, he checked his wristwatch, saw he was on time, and nodded knowingly as though an experiment just completed had produced the expected results. He turned his attention to a copy of *Barron's*.

"Grayson," Pike interrupted. "What's the capacity of this room?"

Grayson lowered the paper. "One hundred and twenty-five, give or take five or ten."

"And how many professionals are there in the New York office?"

"One hundred and forty-eight."

"So who's missing?" said Pike.

Caleb looked more closely at the tables around him. No H&L partners were present.

"That's called executive privilege," said Pike.

Bronson Normby appeared at the edge of the stage and smiled ingratiatingly at the crowd as he crossed to the podium. He blew into the microphone, creating the sound of thunderous surf.

"Works!" said Normby cheerfully. The word crescendoed into a shrill electric whistle, wavered, and, to Normby's consternation, held a particularly piercing note. He was instructed from the floor to take his hand off the mike, which he did. The noise died away. Pike began to clap and others joined him until, blushing, Normby waved for silence.

"Okay, you've had your fun," he said and unconsciously reached out again to touch the mike. Caleb put his hands to his ears just as the speakers squealed. The H&L professionals pounded the tables and roared with laughter.

Shaken, but forcing a small smile, Normby dropped his hands to his sides and launched into his introductory remarks. He said he was sure they had all heard of Expert

Associates, the consultants to consultants. Since founding Expert Associates five years ago Dr. Irving Fine had built an international reputation for his firm, and his list of clients was the envy of the industry. Today's seminar was entitled "TEST," which stood for "The Executive Survival Tactics." The focus would be on decision-making in stress situations and methods of creative problem-solving.

Normby, clapping, said, "Dr. Irving Fine!" and stepped away from the podium.

The President of Expert Associates crossed from stage left, waving to his audience. He warmly shook hands with Normby.

"Thinks he's won an Academy Award," Pike quipped.

Dr. Fine reached deliberately for the microphone. Feedback, raucous applause. Chuckling, he spread his notes over the podium, took a sip of water, and when he had silence began to talk about effective teamwork. He was a round man in his late fifties with the look of a traveling salesman. His suit was robin's-egg blue—too light to qualify as corporate attire. He seemed pleased with himself and pleased to have an audience at his disposal.

Was there a single factor more important to the consultant in the field than the smooth, effective operation of his team? Dr. Fine thought not. The seminar that morning could be classified as a team-dynamics primer, and he hoped they would profit from it. He went on to explain the origin of his theories, describing his application of scientific methodology to management problems and his experiments carried out over the past few years. Today he would take them through an exercise which would help to dramatize his findings.

He signaled to his monitors, who started up the aisles distributing packets of seminar material.

On the cover of the packet was a sketch of the Expert Associates' headquarters on the banks of the Charles River. Caleb removed the contents of the pouch: Dr. Fine's business card; a brochure listing services offered by Expert Associates; two reprints from the *Harvard Business Review* authored by Dr. Fine; and a Xerox of blurbs by business leaders hailing Dr. Fine's "imaginative solution to the problem of the avoidance of the dysfunctional" and "his ability to trigger usable connections from the impractical or the remote and generate operational behaviors." At the bottom of this sheet were a list of awards and citations he had received and a brief synopsis of his academic career.

Dr. Fine invited them to take the materials home and browse through them at their leisure. Then he held up the last two stapled pages which comprised the exercise, slowly reading the instructions. Each foursome was to imagine it was a group of executives in flight from New York to Salt Lake City. Suddenly their plane goes down, crashing in the Utah desert fifty miles north by northwest of the nearest town, killing all aboard except the four members of their group. The plane was off course before it crashed and no SOS was ever radioed. The time is 9:00 a.m. and the temperature is 95° F. and rising. The group salvages the following items from the burning wreck.

—an air map of the region
—a stewardess's cosmetic mirror
—a quart of gin

—a compass
—four pairs of sunglasses
—a prayerbook
—a gallon of water
—a flashlight
—a Swiss Army knife
—four raincoats
—salt tablets
—a loaded revolver
—a paperback book on edible lizards
—a parachute

Their assignment was to number these items—first individually and then as a group—in order of importance to the group's survival. They had ten minutes to complete Part I and twenty minutes for Part II. Dr. Fine cautioned them against discussing the assignment among themselves until every member of the group had completed Part I. He said they could begin.

Caleb removed his mechanical pencil from his breast pocket. Clearly, the first step in the exercise was to decide on a practical course of action. Once that was done, the items could be rated to accommodate that plan. Caleb realized immediately that what he could theorize as a possible solution to the exercise and what he would actually do if stranded in the desert were at odds. Theoretically, he would be foolish to attempt to walk the fifty miles to the nearest town when he had only a quart of water per person and temperatures were certain to rise well over 100° F. At a pace of three miles per hour it would take him seventeen hours of continuous walking. But the alternative—to stay put, pitch a tent using the parachute, and await help— a more conservative, less heroic course of action, required great patience—which he lacked. A third plan, a bit preposterous perhaps, suggested itself a minute later. Existential in its overtones, melodramatic in its execution, it required him to don the raincoat, pour a dry gin martini in the flashlight casement, read aloud from the prayerbook, and ultimately fire a bullet through his head. Nevertheless, he preferred this scenario to roasting in the desert.

He reviewed the items one by one and pondered their relevance. The Swiss Army knife and the gin might be of use if he were bitten by a snake or needed to sterilize a wound, but overall had little value; the same was true for the lizard guide and the prayerbook. Salt tablets had to be either very good for you or very bad. He knew that he would cramp and convulse if he lost too much salt; on the other hand, salt absorbs water and creates dehydration, which was, arguably, the greatest danger. He could see the value of the flashlight if he were to walk in the dark, but if that wasn't the proper course of action, what possible use could he have for it? He wouldn't use it to signal at night because who would send a search party out at night? A trick item, he was sure: rank it high.

Finally he saw what was so ingenious about the exercise. The crisis situation it depicted, with its insistence on the black or white choice of success or failure, its strategic orientation, and its requirement that the material objects provide the only possible salvation, was a conceit for the average business executive's condition. And the beauty of the conceit was that it made no mention of money, as if Dr. Fine meant to say: What has money got to do with an executive's success? Money is merely representational, a symbol of human and material resources. There was some truth to this, Caleb decided. Money was like the textbook definition of energy he had read in a high-school physics course: invisible and yet never irrevocably spent or lost; instead, constantly reallocated and altered in form.

A helicopter, the one he needed to rescue him, whirled up from his stomach. He checked his watch. Five minutes left. So what would he do in the theoretical terms of the exercise, pitch camp or hike out? He decided to be true to his real-life instincts, to be right for the wrong reasons, to defy the boundaries and constraints of the exercise. It *was* what he would do. Wearing the raincoat and sunglasses, armed with pistol and flashlight, he would march south by southeast and lead his people to safety.

He rated the compass first, map second, water third. Next came raincoat, sunglasses, revolver, flashlight, paperback, tablets, mirror, knife, and prayerbook. He listed parachute and gin last.

The others had finished.

Dr. Fine informed them that time was up. They were to begin Part II of the exercise. The members of Caleb's team pulled their chairs closer together.

"I would like you to find me an airline which will fly me to Salt Lake City from New York and get me there at nine a.m.," said Pike. "And do you think I would waste precious time in that kind of heat ranking my belongings?"

"So what *would* you do?" asked Diane.

Pike said he would pitch a tent, using the parachute, and get out of the sun. He spoke as if this were the obvious solution. Grayson and Diane agreed. Diane noted that the parachute would double as a marker which could be spotted from a plane. Outnumbered, Caleb sat quietly and listened. Grayson raised the point that in order to rank the items effectively in the twenty minutes allotted they would need a procedure. He didn't think there was time to vote on every item individually, so he proposed they instead try to achieve a rough consensus. Pike nodded; he said they could begin by picking out the items they felt were most important and ranking them first.

Diane interrupted: she felt their procedure was crude.

"Crude but effective," said Pike.

But Diane felt they should first outline their survival strategy in more detail—that was Step A. For Step B they should discuss generally what items were important and why; Step C, they could stop and assess where they were. And Step D would be to rate the items based on what they had learned. They could spend five minutes on each step.

Pike looked at her in amazement. "And if there is no consensus on the first three steps, we end up wasting three-quarters of our time."

Diane asked Caleb how *he* would like to proceed. Caleb inquired if there wasn't some way they could share and compare their answers to Part I and then explore their differences. He was aware that there was a subjective element at play, but such a procedure would help him to select the best possible answers.

Pike lost his patience. "How are we going to agree on a

procedure? We can't take all of these approaches. We've wasted three minutes already. Somebody is going to have to make the final decisions if we're going to accomplish anything. I have seniority. I propose I do it."

"Why don't we vote on who plays chairperson?" said Diane. "Or draw straws?"

"Next you'll be wanting a party convention."

"He's right," said Grayson. "We're using up time. Let him be chairman."

"Don't you think this is the most important part of the exercise?" asked Diane.

"No, that's wrong. The most important part of the exercise is accurately rating the items. Let's get to work," said Pike.

Grayson seconded the motion.

"We have just witnessed a power play," Diane remarked ruefully.

Pike chose Grayson's seat-of-the-pants approach. He proposed that the raincoats or the parachute be ranked first, cover from the sun being of primary importance. Since they would need the cover of the raincoats while they erected the tent, the raincoats probably should be ranked first. Diane agreed and took the logic a step further: if the raincoats were their first choice of cover, that demoted the parachute's immediate importance. Survival in that first hour depended more on the availability of water.

"Good," said Pike. The group ranked water second.

"Salt," said Pike. "Of vital importance. Without salt you have convulsions and go blind. That's why there's so much salt in Gatorade."

"What about shipwrecked sailors who die from drinking salt water?" asked Diane. "Salt dehydrates you—makes you thirsty."

"Right," said Caleb. He mentioned the effects of salted popcorn.

Pike pooh-poohed the popcorn. "Believe me, salt is important."

Salt was ranked three. Equipped to deal with the heat and sun, the group turned its attention to the long-term problem of survival. They ranked the parachute four, the knife five, the mirror six, the compass seven, and, with time expiring, ranked the last items randomly. The air map had the distinction of being ranked last.

Dr. Fine's voice boomed out at them. Smiling broadly, he ordered them to put down their pencils.

"Everyone's ego intact? Ready for the survival expert's answers?"

According to the expert—and just who this expert was Dr. Fine never said—the item to rank first was the cosmetic mirror. When the plane lost radio contact with the Salt Lake City airport and then failed to appear for its scheduled arrival, a search craft would be sent out promptly. The cosmetic mirror, used as a reflector and signaling device, offered the best hope for their speedy discovery and rescue.

"Plus it enables you to see just how sunburned you've become," Diane whispered.

The raincoats should be ranked second, the gallon of water third. Dr. Fine began an elaborate discussion of the uses a survivor, assuming he had a degree in engineering, could find for a common flashlight. The upshot was the invention of a contraption which resembled an air-conditioner and a water-cooler, fueled by the ammonia in human urine.

"Disgusting," said Diane.

"Unfair," said Caleb.

Salt should be rated last, according to Dr. Fine. "It will kill you."

"I told you so," said Diane.

Caleb imagined Pike forcing his raincoat-clad acolytes to swallow their salt tablets in Jonestown obeisance—only Caleb, who had long since set out on foot, would escape a gruesome death.

Dr. Fine, smug, enjoying the fact he had their attention, went on to give the expert's applications for each item on the list and the rationale for their rankings.

Pike was the first to raise his hand.

"I'll concede that, scientifically speaking, members of my team may have been wrong about the salt tablets, but isn't your ranking of some of these other items a bit subjective?"

"Granted," said Dr. Fine. "But bear with me. The point of this exercise is not to see who can get the highest score. It is, rather, to demonstrate that a solution arrived at collectively is, on average, better than a solution arrived at alone."

He asked them to calculate the difference between each individual's rankings and the expert's rankings and between the team's rankings and the expert's rankings.

"You will find that the group's score will be eight to ten points better—that is, lower—than the average individual score. Not only that, half of the teams in this room will score better than their best individual score. In other words, the safest course of action for the mass of individuals is to do things in a group. QED, there is a justification for the corporation."

In the ballroom antechamber half a dozen waiters in black tie stood at attention behind a long buffet table, prepared to assist in the carving, ladling, and general dispensing of the food. The crowd of suited H&L professionals adjourned for lunch, nosed up to the table to admire the dishes—stunning evidence of the firm's largess. One waiter stirred a caldron of seafood bisque, another feathered juicy slices of beef off a roast. Beyond lay a bronzed turkey on a silver platter, its cavernous belly spilling rich, steaming stuffing. There followed sole bonne femme, chicken cordon bleu, and liver thatched with bacon. Blue Sterno flames licked at stainless-steel pans of mushrooms, stewed onions, green peas. Next came a salmon mousse, a bowl of pink-and-white jointed Gulf shrimp, a plate of sliced tongue and Genoa salami, dishes of egg and potato salad garnished with tomato wedges and parsley, carrot-and-raisin salad, spinach-and-cauliflower salad, cold macaroni salad, Greek and Spanish olives, carrot and celery sticks, radishes and pickle spears. Then came the cakes and pastries, fruits and nuts, and cut-glass bowls filled with sherbet, and to drink, there was a choice of soft drinks or coffee.

After a short grace period in which the food was admired, a tangle of arms reached for plates and the crowd worked its way along the table, sawing at the pale breast of turkey, spearing cold cuts, digging into the bowls of salad. The H&L professionals jostled and jockeyed for shrimp and salmon. The bowl of macaroni salad capsized and a chocolate éclair appeared floating in the stewed onions. A consultant from the Technology Management Group inadvertently slathered Dijon mustard over the front of Caleb's vest, but for the most part order and good manners prevailed.

Grayson had managed to walk away with a pile of roast beef and a generous portion of salmon mousse. By the time Caleb sat down, his friend was halfway through his meal. Diane was not hungry; she had before her a handful of orange carrot sticks. Nibbling indifferently, she hoisted her pocketbook into her lap and rummaged through the contents. Pike sat down proudly holding a plate crowded with neat little piles of food. He reached behind him to pull his chair in snug under him.

"I had to push your colleague Mr. Pridgeon away from the shrimp or he would have taken them all," he said to Caleb and Grayson. He leaned toward Caleb's plate of potato salad, stewed onions, and sole bonne femme. "What a bland-looking meal, Mr. Sparrow."

"What about hers?"

"At least hers has some color to it."

"Onions and sole are two of my favorite foods."

Diane rose and excused herself. A moment later Grayson went up for seconds.

"You like her, don't you?" said Pike.

"Who?"

"Don't 'Who?' me. You're drooling."

"I don't drool."

On Pike's plate each pile had been reduced to a bite-sized morsel. He disposed of these now, one by one. He paused with his fork in the air.

"I have always felt corporations should be single-sexed institutions. There's a special kind of camaraderie found among men when they share the company of other men. Introduce a woman into the group and the men will vie for her attention. Inevitably there is a loss of direction and morale. Why can't women have their own corporations?"

"Forgive me for saying so, but your thinking in this matter is a little primitive."

"See what I mean? Already there is divisiveness."

"Jim, she doesn't have a thing to do with this."

"Admit you like her."

"I like a lot of people at H&L." A bold-faced lie.

"If I find she's interfering with your performance, I'm going to take corrective steps."

"We were arguing the relative merits of women in the office place and now you're lecturing me on what I can and can't do. Jim, there are some things that are none of your business."

"As long as you work for Beauregard and me—very few."

Grayson returned with seconds of salmon mousse. After a silent minute during which Caleb and Pike watched him eat, he looked up from his plate.

"Somebody say something. Don't perpetuate the myth that businessmen are boring."

Dr. Fine, in the opening of the afternoon portion of the seminar, asserted that a team's effectiveness depended on the unique strength of its individual members. These must never be stifled. He asked a series of questions designed to isolate the team-dynamic characteristics which emerged from the Executive Survival Tactics exercise. He spoke of the Chairmanship Assumption Phenomenon, in which a member of the team, in the interest of the group and the assignment, assumed a dominant role and orchestrated the decision-making. This process was a natural, even organic, by-product of team dynamics.

The lecture which followed focused on how to use team dynamics to aid creative problem-solving. Dr. Fine stressed the importance of good manners and a climate of approval in the team discussion and then spent a great deal of time analyzing right- and left-hemisphere thinking and how to encourage brainstorming. His message was clear: be tolerant of the spontaneous, intuitive, and bizarre.

Caleb, Grayson, and Pike, full from lunch, slouched in their chairs, thick-lidded and sleepy, watching Dr. Fine as he outlined the series of experiments he had conducted and their findings.

Diane used the time to write a handful of postcards. Her handwriting was too small for Caleb to read.

Dr. Fine concluded with an impassioned plea for creative solutions to business problems. Only innovation and imagination could keep American business competitive with the Japanese. He concluded by exhorting them to admit "that there is a bit of the artist in all of us!"

"What nonsense," said Pike as the four of them began to collect their belongings.

"Nonsense?" said Diane.

"What you need in this business is math aptitude, an

ability to compute and decipher numbers. And, frankly, that's why men are better at it than women."

"Better?" said Diane, temper mounting.

"Men have higher math aptitudes than women. Everyone knows that."

"That's a myth."

"You think so? Then tell us what you scored on the GMATs. I bet Caleb here scored higher than you did."

"I haven't taken them," said Caleb.

"What I scored is none of your business. Besides, quantitative ability can be learned. What's most important in business—or anything else—is character. And you are walking proof that *that* can't be learned."

"Listen, little lady, this is no debutante cotillion."

"Call it off, you two," said Grayson.

"A truce," said Caleb.

"Fine, this is like arguing with an ill-mannered third-grader."

Pike laughed and shook his head. "Okay, I surrender."

"Let's share a cab," said Diane to Caleb.

"Caleb, you've got a lot of work to do for me. Don't stay out too late," said Pike.

"I can take care of myself."

"And I wouldn't lay a hand on her. She probably knows karate."

"Mind your own business," said Caleb sullenly.

He followed Diane from the ballroom, unable to take his eyes off the alluring hitch of hips ahead of him.

14.

Findings

CALEB made a series of findings about Diane that evening in her studio apartment.

Finding No. 1: She had definite likes and dislikes.

Dot. Her likes included:

Dash. Tidiness. There were no dishes in her sink, no dust on her windowsills. On her shelves, art books and hardback editions of Joyce, Forster, Eliot, and other moderns were arrayed according to size. Every picture— a framed poster of a Degas and another of a Hopper and two American landscapes, one by Church and one by Cole—was perfectly centered. The entire apartment looked brand new and spotless.

Dash. Backgammon. Her favorite game. She had made her own set out of an antique breadboard. In the high spirits of kids playing hooky from school, they sat on her worn Persian carpet, Diet Pepsis at their sides, rolling through game after game, her moves deft and sure, his pondered and marched out, until at fifty cents a point she had won twelve dollars off him.

Dash. Chinese food. Specifically: egg rolls, sweet-and-sour soup, dry-fried string beans, and moo shoo pork. They ordered the meal by phone and had it delivered. He paid the delivery boy, who was no more Chinese than they were—paid him out of her winnings.

Dash. Red wine. A 1974 Châteauneuf du Pape, the case a gift from her father on her last birthday. An oenophile, her father attributed great restorative qualities to wine. She slit the foil, peeled it back with the corkscrew blade, smiling at him in a way that sent a ripple of wonder through him. She twisted the screw deep into the cork and, planting the bottle on the carpet between her crossed legs, pried the cork up and out with two squeaks. She sniffed it, sniffed the bottle. A ruby rivulet joined the bottle to the glass. She peered at him through its swishing translucence and dipped her nostrils to the rim. A sip. She handed him the glass. The wine rolled back into his mouth and lay between his tongue and palate. He swallowed and could taste the berryishness in his sinuses.

Dot. Her dislikes included:

Dash. Arrogant men. By which she meant Jim Pike. What was it, she asked, which made these fast-trackers think they were so important? They should be required to earn a Master's in modesty.

Dash. Her mother. For favoring her sister. Sally was

two years younger than Diane and yet Mrs. Landry was forever asking Diane why she couldn't be more like her sister, who was pretty, social, and had none of Diane's "tendencies." This infuriated Diane, who pointed out to her mother that Sally, the graduate of a junior college, had only the semblance of a job working for the Junior League. Diane didn't condemn her sister for being what she was—Tiffany marriage material—but she herself did not want to smile for a living.

Caleb took a swallow of wine. His parents might favor him, his father certainly did, but wasn't there tact in their preference? Still, he felt uncomfortable with the closeness of the parallel.

Dash. Politics. Her father was a well-known Washington attorney who loved to argue politics and always prefaced his remarks by saying, "I'm a Republican. What, by the way, are you?" She was neither. In her opinion, both parties were ineffectual and self-serving. She had resolved to ignore the national elections.

Dash. Depression. Sometimes she became so depressed that she had trouble breathing, the pressure concentrating itself on her chest like a sack of concrete. The Big Sadness, she called it; she could accidentally trigger a spell by forgetting a name, losing something, or arguing with her mother. She was convinced this susceptibility to depression was a character flaw.

"I'm a psychological weakling, and the only way to overcome this disability is by discipline and concentration. That business with Pike today? That's good for me. I need adversity. I need humiliation to help me build calluses.

As I figure it, I don't have to like him to profit from working with him. I was thinking of requesting a project with him, just for my psychological development."

Finding No. 2: Diane considered herself an oddball.

She said she didn't belong either to the art world or the business world. She was a misfit because she was too smart, too weirdly, apolitically intellectual. Did he know what it was like to be twenty-seven and generally known as an oddball?

That meant three years separated them, not the two he had thought. Three years made her profoundly older in a way two years did not, and yet, as measured by post-teen years, not by any means an older woman. He wished he could say the only meaningful difference in their ages was an MBA and one promotion. But three years: the difference would be noticed, commented upon if he continued to date her.

Finding No. 3: She was sexy for an oddball.

Dot. She drank the lion's share of the wine and leaned her head back against the couch, exposing her delicate neck.

Dot. She decided she wanted a back rub.

Dot. Seated on the cushion of her butt, he plunged his hands under her shirt and closed his eyes at the surprise of her skin under his palms. He kneaded the muscles in her neck, between her shoulderblades, and down into the pit at the base of her spine. Then he worked his way back up, drumming with his fists. When the shirt interfered, she said, "Here," and arched up under him, reached back, and drew the blouse off. The raisin of a nipple swung into view. She lay bare-backed before him, and he began again, curiously breathless. How skinny she was! He could count her ribs, and there was a bump for each vertebra. Under his hand he felt the tom-tom of her heart and wondered if he should attribute the quick beat to hypertension or the thick pulse of desire. The thought was enough to make a familiar fern unfold inside him, and minutes later he interrupted his karate chops and finger prods to pinch an unruly muscle of his own.

But if he had dreams of sweaty wrestling and promiscuous gymnastics, and if he assumed one discarded article of clothing would follow another—and he did, so much so that he discreetly unknotted his necktie and thumbed his top three shirt buttons through their eyelets—Diane was to disappoint him by quietly dropping off to sleep, her jaw twisted to one side, her lovely mouth ajar. He rose and tiptoed to her closet to hang up her blouse; he spread the louvered doors. Under a shelf of folded sweaters, a rainbow of cable-stitched cardigans and crew necks and Fair Isles, hung the outfits of Diane's life: the suits so remarkably like his own—gray and blue wools and poplins; a black velvet evening gown to be worn with pearls; something frilly and turquoise which must have been a bridesmaid dress; then the cotton print dresses of summer and half a dozen skirts. At the end of the row he found two girlish nighties, one flecked with tiny dancing ponies and the other striped with rows of cherries.

He scraped apart the hangers and stepped in among the folds of material—something he had done in his mother's closet as a boy. He hugged some of the dresses and sniffed the Chanel No. 5 of bygone evenings, pained to think Diane had a whole history which he knew nothing about.

Cushioned in Diane's wardrobe, warm and cozy, musing

over his findings of the evening, he came upon one of his very own: he was in love with her. He knew it because although she was there, just twenty feet from him, he missed her terribly. The certainty of his discovery, and the relief attendant on it, brought tears to his eyes.

What to do about this sudden love? He considered waking her to make a romantic proclamation, but it seemed too early in their relationship for that. He could sit and watch her, but the inner turmoil would be too much. Finally, he decided to sneak out and let her sleep.

He left his space among the clothes hangers and pulled a blanket off the top shelf and draped it over her. He retrieved his briefcase and, after checking to be sure the door would lock behind him, pulled it closed.

The doorman remarked that it was a fine evening.

"You bet it is," replied the jubilant lover.

15.

Robert Redux

"CALEB, I panicked."

There in the hall of his apartment stood a tall, bearded man in a wrinkled blue Oxford-cloth shirt and gray sweat pants who looked remarkably like his brother.

"I had five cocktails on the red-eye. Five. I thought they'd help me sleep. They didn't. And do you know how many years it's been since I had a drink? I'm a mess, Caleb, and you were the one person I knew I could talk to. For God's sake, don't tell anyone I'm here."

"How long have you been like this?" asked Caleb, concerned.

"A week or so. I know what's wrong with me. This is my first adult crisis. I've never had one before."

"Seems like an anxiety attack."

"Exactly."

"What can I do for you?"

"Put me to bed."

Caleb picked up Robert's duffel bag and moved it into his bedroom, then began to strip the bed. Robert sat in Caleb's desk chair and drank a beer in gulps. "Your room-mate gave me this," he said, holding up the empty bottle. "Then he split. Figured I wanted to be alone. Seemed like a nice guy."

"He means well."

"California used to be full of people like that. Don't ask me what happened to them all. I think they pulled that lemming trick and fell into the Pacific. Now the state is full of disenchanted New Yorkers."

Caleb straightened up, pleased with his hospital corners. Robert flopped onto the bed. He raised a shoe and had Caleb unlace it for him. He slowly unbuttoned his shirt and dropped it on the floor. He had a farmer's tan—face, neck, and arms—and his chest was a babyish white; a jiggly little belly sagged over the elastic of his sweat pants.

"It's nice and cool in here."

"You want me to leave the AC on?"

"Sure. I like the sound."

"How about some hot milk?"

Robert yawned. "Maybe half a glass."

With the steaming mug of milk in hand, Caleb returned to his room to find his brother sitting up in bed, sniffing.

"What's that smell?"

"What smell?"

"Your apartment has a bad smell."

"Socks?"

"Like something died in the walls."

"I don't smell it."

"Nasty."

Caleb gave Robert the mug and sat in the desk chair.

"How's Dad?"

"Seems okay."

"And the Bitch of Buchenwald?"

"She's Swiss, not German. She's in Zurich."

"Do they know yet? About my engagement?"

"I don't think so. When did you mail the letter?"

"Yesterday."

"Well, what did you expect?"

"You didn't tell them?"

"I haven't said a word."

Robert rolled the warm mug in his hands.

"How's that milk?"

"Good. Hot."

"Feel better?"

"A bit. I've got dyspepsia."

"Dyspepsia?"

"Bad stomach. Makes you flatulent."

"I thought she was a nutritionist."

"She is. Can't cook."

"Is she pretty?"

"Looks like Katherine Ross." His eyes brightened. "She really does."

For a moment neither said a word. Caleb considered telling Robert about Diane but decided the moment was not right. And, after all, how much was there to tell other than that he had given her a backrub?

"So what's up with you?" asked Robert, reading his thoughts.

"Not much. Work."

"Is that all you do?"

"It's all I have time for."

"Work interesting?"

"Kind of. How's the God Squad?"

"The Wave? People keep joining."

"I'm glad."

"We can't house them all, so we're taking day students."

"Still excited about the work?"

"Did you think I was in it for the money?"

Caleb laughed and they fell silent.

"She know you're gone?"

"Does by now."

"Want to call her?

"Nope. . . . It's not just the wedding."

"The church?"

"No, not just the church."

"California."

"Nope."

"Then what?"

"Fatherhood," said Robert, patting his stomach.

"No kidding!"

"No kidding."

"How did it happen?"

"I hope you're joking."

"No, no. I mean isn't she on the pill?"

"She doesn't believe in it. She's a Wave Fundamentalist."

"What about foams and gels?"

"Don't be disgusting."

"Do you feel too young to have kids?"

"Too old. I'm jaded."

"You'll make a great pop."

"I have no patience and I'll be too strict. My son will grow up to despise me."

He shut his eyes and grimaced. "I mean, what if he likes Led Zeppelin?"

"Not much you can do about it."

"Or computers. That would kill me."

"Try to think about the fun you'll have."

"But I'm so unprepared."

"Think," said Caleb. "A boy of your own."

"Golf. What if he wants to play golf?"

"I'll take him bird-watching."

"Not a jock. Please don't let him be a jock."

Robert handed back the empty mug and slid down in bed.

"A little boy who loves you," said Caleb, leaning forward.

"Sure are nice when they're little."

"Waving his arms," said Caleb, waving his arms.

"Wants to be picked up."

"A good little kid."

"A damn good kid," said Robert, smiling.

"More milk?"

"No, thanks. Guess I'll hit the hay."

"Good to have you here."

"Caleb?"

"Yes, Robert?"

"We should talk, Caleb."

"Sure, Robert. We'll talk."

16.

Rumor

ARLY the next morning Caleb lay awake on the Castro convertible paralyzed with dread. How could it be Friday already? The presentation was on Wednesday morning and he had accomplished nothing! What did he think he was doing? This was not just his job he was treating with such nonchalance—it was his career!

The first news he heard upon arriving at H&L was that Grayson had been promoted. Grayson sat at his desk, his freckled face looking enormously pleased.

"They didn't want to make me a consultant—not without an MBA. So instead I'm the assistant to the Vice Chairman. How do you like that?"

The phone interrupted them, a well-wisher who had just heard the news. Grayson laughed into the receiver, and Caleb, excited for Grayson, walked back to his desk wondering what, if anything, this meant for the other researchers and—it was admittedly a selfish consideration— what it meant for him.

Pike, who had returned to the office after the TEST seminar and worked through the night, burst into the researchers' room, red-eyed and rumpled, to check on Caleb's progress.

Caleb covered his desk with his hands and pleaded to be left alone. Pike rationalized out loud that if Caleb was reluctant to show him his work, it meant he was not satisfied, maybe ashamed of it. Under those circumstances it was imperative Caleb show him what he had done because they had no time left to fool around. Caleb capitulated.

"Is that all you've done? Where's your aggressiveness, Caleb? Your professional hard-on?"

"Do you mind not using language like that in here? There's nothing professional about obscenity."

"Look who's talking. You're the one who's brought sex into the office place."

"I don't know what you're talking about."

"Just do the work, Caleb." Pike slammed the door on his way out.

Grayson leaned out from his cubicle. "Pervert!"

For the sake of thoroughness, Pike wanted Caleb to analyze long-term versus short-term compensation to see if the mix was right. Specifically, Caleb had to determine how much each of the top Benefact Corp officers had earned from the stock-option plan over the past five years. By reading six years of proxy statements Caleb worked out the number and value of the awards at the time of grant, their number and value at the time they were exercised, and then calculated the value earned and the value of the awards outstanding; these figures had to be annualized. The difficulty arose from the fact that stock splits and stock dividends had to be backed out of these figures before he began. Plus there were strange, unaccounted-for awards and indecipherable provisions to take into consideration; in some cases a participant was dropped from a plan, or the plan itself was dropped and a new one introduced in its place.

One of the greatest challenges was mastering the terminology. How did a non-qualified stock option differ from a qualified one? How did a stock option differ from a stock appreciation right? What was a performance share, or, for that matter, a performance unit? Most mysterious of all was the phantom stock plan. As far as Caleb was concerned, they were all phantom stock plans—so technical they eluded understanding.

Furthermore, since Caleb's objective was to determine if the mix of short- and long-term compensation was fair, he had to have something to compare it against, and this meant looking at the six years of proxies for every company in the comparative sample. When Caleb calculated the number of hours it had taken him to analyze the Benefact Corp plans, and multiplied that by the number of companies in the sample, the figure came to over a hundred hours, or two weeks' work. Caleb had all of two working days. It was then he first heard a strange animal noise beside him and, looking around, realized it was the sound of his own panting.

Diane dropped in for a visit at 12:30 and kissed Caleb

on the cheek. "Thanks to your ministrations last night, I slept like a log."

A gasp from Pridgeon.

"What did I do with my shirt? I couldn't find it this morning."

A second gasp, as though a pipe had burst.

"I hung it in your closet."

The phone rang and Diane plucked it off the hook. "Mr. Sparrow's office. . . . Oh, good afternoon, Mr. Tapolletti." She put the inflection on the "afternoon," her voice a cheerful warble. She glanced at Caleb; he grimaced.

"Why, no, Mr. Tapolletti. Mr. Sparrow is not in the office at the moment. He is at AT&T. And then he will be lunching with Senator D'Amato. Perhaps I could have him return your call early next week. . . . Yes. It's in the mail."

She hung up with a laugh.

"You're off the hook, but don't thank me. Thank Alfonse D'Amato. The only Italian-American name I could think of off the top of my head."

"So there are some advantages to being a female executive."

"None that I'll admit to. See you later."

Jamie appeared at his elbow seconds after Diane left. "I happened to pick up on that call. Secretaries are just a big joke with her, aren't they?"

"Administrative assistants," Caleb corrected.

"She ought to try it."

"She did me a favor."

"Many, I bet. I'm sure she's very liberal with her favors."

"Do I detect a jealous note?"

"I've just had enough of these Mary Cunningham types. Why should I feel inadequate?"

Caleb skipped lunch. In the afternoon he and Grayson took a long coffee break and discussed Pike's workaholism, insensitivity, and failure to delegate responsibility—shortcomings they were determined to avoid.

"You've got to be aware of other people's feelings," said Grayson. "Otherwise, you become dehumanized."

"Let me ask you something," Caleb lowered his voice. "Do you notice a difference in *me?*"

"I don't. Jamie says she does. She says she can recognize pre-coital behavior just from posture. She was an anthro major in college."

"She said that?" said Caleb, stiffening.

There had to be some visible differences; why should they be limited to a sparkle in the eye? And he knew better than to think love was ennobling. It was far more accurate to say love made you spastic.

"Grayson, if you want to celebrate your promotion tonight with Jamie and skip the boxing match, my father will understand."

"We had our little celebration at lunch."

"Where did you take her?"

"To a travel agent. We booked a flight to San Francisco for the third week in September. She wants to visit the vineyards during the fall harvest, and I want to sit in on some classes at Stanford. We're not going to waste our money on a lot of extravagant celebrating. I'm going to the fight with you."

Two consultants congratulated Caleb, passing him in the

hall. At first he assumed they had mistaken him for Grayson. When it happened again and the consultant, a reputed playboy in the Government Services Group, leered at him and winked knowingly, Caleb realized that the worst had happened: he had been credited with the seduction of Diane and, from all appearances, was something of a hero for it. Pridgeon, that jerk, was spreading rumors. Caleb wondered if, under those circumstances, he should avoid being seen with Diane, but when he went into the lounge for a cup of coffee, she was there depositing coins in a vending machine.

"I can't get used to these things coming out of a machine." She held up an apple. Her first bite left a deep white cavity. "Tastes the same."

In walked Pike, his vest unbuttoned and his shirt sleeves rolled up to the elbows. As he veered toward them, Diane looked down at her apple.

"There's the goddess Diane—virgin huntress, protectress of women, mathematical marvel!" he drawled. As Diane took a second bite, he pinched her bottom. Her riposte, a top-spin forehand, began at her waist and rose as she straightened her elbow and swung around; her open palm met his left cheek with a smack and jerked his head a quarter-turn to the right. Without looking back, she brushed past him and marched out of the lounge.

Blood streamed from Pike's nose.

"I'm bleeding!" he said, amazed.

Seated in a chair Caleb found for him, his head thrown back, breathing through his mouth, he needed assurance that he didn't have blood on his tie.

"I bleed easily," he confided. "But don't tell her that."

When the bleeding stopped, Caleb walked with him to his office.

"Yes, sir, I think you've got some competition, lover boy. I think she likes me."

"She can't stand you."

"Oh, now, Caleb, I don't see why we can't share her. I think I should staff her on our next assignment. She's supposed to be very good at client-handling. And I like my client handled."

Caleb went to Diane's office to tell her Pike was being a good sport and not to worry.

"Now I've done it. I've jeopardized my career because I couldn't control myself. I'm too emotional—I've got to learn to be cool and dispassionate and masculine."

"If you want to be masculine, you shouldn't slap him. You should slug him."

"Very funny, Caleb."

Diane sat in her swivel chair hugging her pocketbook to her chest like a teddy bear. "He wants to force me out —you know that, don't you? Nothing would give him greater satisfaction than to see me fired. And now I've given him an excuse."

"He thinks you like him."

"That's preposterous."

"You underestimate his vanity. He loves to get your attention. I would swear he enjoyed that bloody nose."

"He didn't say anything about firing me?"

"Just the opposite. He's flirting with the idea of staffing you on one of his assignments. Diane, if you're that worried about him, why don't you just pretend to like him?"

"Pretend?"

"Yes, act."

"That's what *you* do?"

"To some extent, yes."

"To what extent?"

"There are people here I pretend I like—that researcher Pridgeon, for example. Sometimes I pretend I like the work I'm doing when I don't. I even pretend I'm happy when I'm not."

"I don't do that. I'd be afraid of forgetting how I truly felt."

"That's the whole point."

"You have to be a good pretender."

"Yes, you do."

"I'm a lousy pretender."

"Diane, I have to get back to work. Would you like to go bird-watching in Central Park tomorrow morning?"

"You're a bird-watcher?"

"I used to be very serious about it. Now I've forgotten most of what I knew."

"Like me with my painting. Sure, I'd love to go. I've never been."

H&L on a Friday afternoon in the summer was a place of frenzied activity. The reception area became an obstacle course of suitcases and hanger bags and parachute-cloth duffels. The partners left at lunch to get a head start on the weekend. By 3:30 the firm's code of professional conduct had been suspended: neckties came off; secretaries called bosses by their first names; shouts and farewells echoed down the hallways. In this milieu Caleb had trouble concentrating.

He looked at the symbols on the face of the calculator and the numbers displayed in red, and for a moment they meant nothing to him. Were these numbers projected or actual? What was he supposed to be doing with them? —378.25. Negative? The number didn't look right. He solved for the slope. The calculator threw up its hands in a display of nines. And then he remembered he was no longer running regressions; he was evaluating stock options. Sitting on the edge of his chair he started over in a state of irritability and panic—the only mind-set in which he successfully avoided mistakes.

He left work at 4:45 after arranging for Grayson to meet him at Yorkville Place. To avoid the Friday-afternoon crush in Grand Central—commuters and weekenders bound for Upstate and the Berkshires—Caleb walked north on Park toward 59th Street, where at the far end of the subway platform he hoped to find a space on the express.

He had just stepped up to the curb on 57th Street when a policeman appeared and motioned him to stay where he was. Caleb started to raise his arms, thinking that on top of everything he was under arrest. But there were cops on every corner, halting the traffic and pedestrian flow on Park Avenue and clearing 57th Street. Within a minute they had brought the traffic on one of the city's busiest intersections to a complete standstill. Across 57th Street roared a squad of white-helmeted police on motorcycles. A military coup, thought Caleb. After them there was nothing for the space of a block. Caleb craned his neck to see down the street. At last a second swarm of motorcycles and a wide, low limousine streaked by. Caleb saw a tiny

white hand in the rear side window, waving. He made a
mental note to check the evening papers to see who it
was. Twenty minutes later the coup was forgotten; he had
more important matters on his mind.

"Caleb, I don't like what I see around here. Someone
left the TV on this morning and the lights in the hall, and
the kitchen tap was dripping." Robert was sitting up in
Caleb's bed, a Bible in his lap.

"We don't pay for the utilities."

"That's not the point. It's wasteful. And go look at
the food in your refrigerator. Doughnuts, pizza, grape
juice, Tab, ketchup, mayonnaise. That stuff is loaded with
carcinogens. You may have little tumors already. Caleb,
if I were you, I'd get out of here. Leave the city. You're
living in your own little Love Canal." He straightened the
sheet over his knees. "It's ironic, really. I came here seeking
your help and now I realize that it's my duty to help *you*."

Caleb sat down in his desk chair, exasperated. "Robert,
I know you mean well, but I don't want to be rescued or,
for that matter, converted."

"Convert you! I beg your pardon! I'm not some bus-
station hustler!"

"No, I know you're not. Forget I said it."

"I'm no proselytizer."

"Of course not."

"You hurt my feelings, Caleb."

"I said I'm sorry. I've had a long day."

"Christians have feelings, too, you know."

"Drop it, Robert!" Caleb looked at his watch. "Dad is

expecting me at six thirty. Dale's coming and so is a friend from work. Sure you won't join us?"

Robert was sure. He stretched out his legs and stared through the window at the hazy blue June sky.

"I intend to spend the evening in celestial contemplation."

17.

The Garden

GRAYSON arrived promptly at six o'clock, and he and Caleb, both wearing jackets and ties, split a beer while they waited for Dale to finish dressing. After brief introductions Robert returned to Caleb's room, where he could be heard muttering as he read aloud from Ezekiel.

"Do *not* mention to my father that Robert's in New York," Caleb warned his friends as they rode the elevator to the lobby. "Robert's in hiding."

"The guy is a little wacko," said Dale to Grayson by way of explanation.

Horatio, a powerfully built black Olympus Brands chauffeur who knew jujitsu, leaned against the hood of the indigo Lincoln Continental outside the Sutton Place apartment building where Bob and Gretchen Sparrow lived. He was reviewing the day's race results with Benedict, a diminutive Swedish doorman better known as Eggs. Caleb had known them both for years and knew that unless they had an argument their evening chat did not, in either's opinion, constitute a true conversation; but if they disagreed, which they much preferred, and if they haggled over horses, greyhounds, politics, or the weather, their day would be complete. They conceded points grudgingly, and at Christmas each gave the other a bottle of Scotch.

When Caleb's cab pulled up, Eggs opened the car door and saluted each of the young men in turn. Horatio tipped his chauffeur's cap to Caleb, raised his fists to his chin, and jabbed.

"Are we taking that thing to the Garden?" asked Dale. "Now, that's class."

Caleb wished Dale would lower his voice.

Bob and Gretchen Sparrow's penthouse apartment had one exceptional feature, a brick terrace with a southern exposure and a view of the East River. It was here, weather permitting, that Gretchen entertained at lunch the wives of other successful executives along with the wives of ambassadors from a select group of Western European nations—she couldn't abide the French. And it was here she had recently been photographed by *W*. It seemed to Caleb that Gretchen's greatest disappointment as a member of the Sparrow family was that nobody gave her credit for having money of her own.

The rest of the apartment was spacious and Scandinavian in design. The furniture was all bare wood or of tubular stainless-steel construction. There were mirrors everywhere and the ashtrays looked too precious to use.

The only room that gave any evidence of his father's presence was the study with its fireplace, mahogany desk, zebra-skin rug, and bookcase of best-sellers. It was here that Bob Sparrow had his collection of golf trophies— four shelves of what he affectionately called his "hardware": a row of silver bowls the size of German helmets, inscribed plates standing on their rims, pewter mugs, a silver-plated golf ball, martini shakers, and statuettes of bronze golfers—clubs raised in the backswing—mounted on miniature pedestals.

"So your old man is a jock," said Dale when he saw the collection.

"Captain of the team at Brown," said Caleb, not without pride.

"Warm in here," said Dale, disguising a plea for a cocktail.

Caleb went to look for beers. The refrigerator was virtually empty; clearly, his father had done no shopping since Gretchen left. Caleb returned to the study empty-handed. His father had finished showering and stood before the trophy case buttoning his cuffs.

"Golf has done more for my career than any degree could. I wish I could get Caleb to play. Frankly, I would much rather pay for golf lessons than business school. Either of you play?"

Dale nodded vigorously and mentioned the Baltusral course in New Jersey. Bob Sparrow said he had played in a Pro-Am there a few years back.

"Yes indeed. I've been telling Caleb that his name could be on some of these trophies if he would just learn the sport. There have always been fine golfers in my family. Do you play, Grayson?"

"No, sir. But I wish I did." Grayson stared with longing at a silver plate inscribed, "Westchester C.C., Best Ball, 1st Place, 1965."

"Dad, Horatio's waiting," said Caleb, fidgeting.

Horatio was sick with envy. "Shoot, Mr. Sparrow. You ever get extra tickets to the fights, you let Horatio know."

Bob Sparrow laughed and said he would see what he could do.

"Don't I always pay you?"

"Yes, you do, Horatio. But if you made better bets, you wouldn't have to."

"Tonight I win. I got my money on the Python tonight."

"Is that Malone or Dawson?"

Horatio slapped the steering wheel, amazed that anyone could have ringside seats for a title bout between Pedro "Python" Malone and Bobo Dawson and not know the fighters' nicknames.

"Malone Dawson—he's mean, but he's a bleeder. Hope you ain't in the front row."

"Tenth row," said Bob Sparrow, removing his wallet to check the tickets. He sat in the front seat beside Horatio so that the three boys could sit together in the back. Caleb could see the pleasure in his father's face when Dale remarked, "This is something!" His father believed the limousine ride would be a huge treat for them, and instructive: a way of letting them taste the rewards of commitment and hard work. Caleb feared that his father would require constant reassurance that nothing had gone unappreciated. He began to feel the fun leak out of the evening.

Grayson struck up a conversation with Mr. Sparrow, probing his opinions on the flight of corporations to the suburbs, the growth of the financial-services industry, and the role of the SEC. Bob Sparrow paraded out his opinions, in a measured voice, wagging his index finger as he reminded them of the dangers of excessive regulation, adroitly turning Grayson's questions into questions of his own.

When the limousine glided past two young women strolling arm in arm, Dale nudged Caleb, pointed to his crotch, and raised his eyebrows. Caleb tried to ignore him and concentrate on what Grayson was saying about the collapse of the high-volume standardization system of production.

Instead of delivering them to a four-star restaurant as Caleb had hoped, the limousine drove them directly to Madison Square Garden. Bob Sparrow had forgotten about his offer to take them out to dinner, Caleb realized, a hot flush rushing to his head.

Their seats were perfect. Bob Sparrow sat on one end, Dale beside him, Caleb next, and Grayson on the aisle. Beams of spotlights cut through a haze of tobacco smoke and lit up and enlarged the taut ropes and the white canvas of the ring. Only a few women were scattered through the crowd, but there were men of all sorts from those clad in mink Mao jackets and wide-brimmed fedoras to those in muscle shirts and rugby shorts. These were men to whom Caleb could attribute no profession.

Dale volunteered to get the first round of franks and

beer; he pushed past them to the stairs. Bob Sparrow leaned over the empty seat and explained to Grayson in a hearty tone that he often tired of dining in restaurants and that sometimes nothing tasted better than a frankfurter. Grayson answered politely that he knew what Mr. Sparrow meant. Caleb winced. Would Grayson think his father cheap? This whole outing was a wretched idea, Caleb decided, prickles of perspiration spreading across his brow.

Dale reappeared holding out a cardboard tray of beers and mustard-smeared hot dogs wrapped in greasy paper. He had bought two extra franks; Bob Sparrow ate them both.

In the first fight two Hispanic boys squared off and immediately began to pelt each other with punches to the head, neither making much effort to defend himself in his eagerness to strike a crippling blow. They were so similar in size and build and so evenly matched that they could have passed for brothers. Caleb referred to the program and gave a start when he read that they *were* brothers. Neither Grayson nor Dale found this in the least remarkable.

Between rounds a chick in hot pants slinked around the ring holding up the round number. Dale found her as exciting as the fight and stood to blow kisses, an antic which made Bob Sparrow give a howl of laughter. By the tenth round the two weary pugilists shuffled around the ring hugging each other, now and then wrestling free an arm to sock the other in the ribs. Finally the boxer in the white shorts lost consciousness and slid through the other's arms to the canvas.

Grayson bought the beers. Dale climbed out to stretch his legs and returned with a second round of frankfurters. To Caleb's dismay, his father ate one more.

"Let me reimburse you," Caleb whispered to Dale and Grayson. "I know it's getting expensive."

"No, Caleb," said Dale, supremely satisfied with his contribution to the evening. "It's my pleasure." Grayson, too, refused the offer.

In the second bout a tall, sinewy black fighter named Henderson skipped around his opponent, a slow and solid white fighter, Marcus, by executing a complex series of dips and ducks and feints. The burly white fighter revolved slowly like a gun turret and punched Henderson in the forehead. When it happened a second time, Henderson snorted and shook his head and gave a white mouthguard grin. He stuck his head out and jeered at Marcus, only to take a clobbering shot in the left ear which pitched him onto his side on the canvas. During the referee's count Henderson managed to draw his knees up under him until he crouched on all fours, his head slowly pitching from side to side. The referee declared Marcus the winner.

It was agreed that concession-stand beers didn't hold their chill. They had to be drunk quickly or they became an undrinkable saliva-like juice. Whenever Caleb finished one cup, Dale or Grayson, the purveyors, pushed a fresh one into his hand. By the fifth round of the title fight the light in the Garden had adopted an amber tint and Caleb's bladder ached.

Grayson and Dale had switched places, and although Caleb couldn't hear what Grayson was discussing with

Bob Sparrow, he was depressed to think his friends were deliberately sharing the responsibility, the chore, of entertaining his father.

The noise during the title bout was an ocean roar. It began as Malone and Dawson, robed and hooded, worked their way up the aisle to the ring, and then swelled as each in turn circled the ring, arms raised, skin gleaming with sweat and oils.

Bobo Dawson outscored "Python" Malone in the early rounds by bulldozing the champion into the ropes and working the body. Malone, however, was a disciplined fighter and he had a fast jab. He began to tie up Dawson every time Dawson crowded in on him. In one quick exchange he cut Dawson's eyebrow with a hook, and the Romans around Caleb went wild. A minute later Dawson managed to hammer Malone straight in the face. A shingle snapped—the nose broke.

Between the tenth and eleventh rounds Caleb, dizzy as if he himself had absorbed a blow, left his chair on the pretense of going to the bathroom. He was hot, feverishly so, and close to fainting, and he tripped on the second step. Grayson started up after him. Caleb waved him away, and, holding his stomach where he hurt the most, he began the slow climb to the nearest exit. I'm drunk, he thought. The outing has been a disaster. Above him the crowd shouted and waved their fists and seemed to taunt him. In the ring Malone's uppercut had jackknifed into Dawson's chin and staggered the fighter. Caleb wandered on through the cries of elation, bleary-eyed and humbled at his expulsion from the Garden.

* * *

Horatio and the limousine were waiting at the curb on Penn Plaza. Bob Sparrow shook hands with Caleb's friends and, to Caleb's surprise, slipped him fifty dollars to "have some fun."

"Your dad is a great guy. I didn't expect him to be so easygoing," said Dale.

"I'll second that. He's an impressive man."

"You think so?" said Caleb, brightening.

"I can see why he ended up CEO of Olympus Brands," said Grayson.

"Well, he just handed me fifty bucks, so let's do something!" Caleb had recovered enough to go on.

"I've got a place," said Dale and repeated the assertion as he started north on Eighth Avenue, Caleb and Grayson following.

Dale took them to a strip joint in Times Square. Caleb paid the cover and the three young men were granted access to a dim room where colored lights played on four square elevated dance floors, each roughly twice the size of a Ping-Pong table. At each dance floor the patrons sat with their elbows propped on the table's padded rim, eyes fixed on the contortions of the stripper before them. Smiling wickedly and rubbing his hands together, Dale walked up to the nearest table, straightened three empty chairs, and tucked himself into the middle one. Caleb and Grayson sat down on either side of him.

Dale waved to the stripper. "Her name's Becky."

The stripper looked about seventeen. She had white skin, long, fine hair dyed gold, and the requisite large breasts. Her vest and skirt had been discarded before they arrived. Now she unfastened her black lace brassiere and swung it over her head in wide circles. She didn't so much dance as gyrate—first her head, swinging her mop of hair from side to side, then spinning her tassels and last revolving her limber hips. Most of this she did with her eyes closed, so Caleb didn't see that they were the color of Navajo turquoise until the music changed and she did a split, bringing her body to eye level. She had a serious face.

From a sitting position she rolled onto her side to do an elegant leg-lift. Off came her panties. Then she sprawled onto her stomach and her movement became syncopated. She arched her back and, while executing a slow push-up, let her fanny bob up and down, touching her G-string to the surface of the table on each dip. To Caleb all this was more acrobatic than erotic.

Dollar bills began to appear on the vinyl cushions. She crawled from one to the next, wiggling her backside, touching a breast to a nose or, if the bill was more than a single, thrusting her G-string at him.

Dale removed a ten from his wallet, creased it along its length, and lay it like a green tent on the padding before him. "Watch this, you guys!" He signaled to Becky, forming a one and a zero with his fingers. She smiled at him— her teeth needed straightening—then she lowered her breasts into his face. He laughed and tried to nibble one. She grabbed him by the hair and hugged his head to her chest. Rising to a squat, she placed the bill in his teeth and brought her G-string level with his nose. Then she lowered the G-string a few inches with two fingers and allowed him to tuck the bill into this makeshift purse.

An arm shot out. Grayson, in a rage, pushed Dale over. Dale floundered as the chair scraped and crashed under him.

"You're sick!" yelled Grayson.

Becky, covering her breasts with one arm, slid away from them. Dale grabbed Grayson around the knees and tried to uproot him. It took two bouncers to separate them.

On the sidewalk outside, Dale called Grayson a fascist.

"Fine. Better a fascist than a pervert!"

"Obviously, you've never been to a striptease before. You don't appreciate the art form."

"That girl is a child."

"She's a hooker, you jerk!"

"What she was doing was demeaning."

"She gets plenty for it, believe me."

The mention of money had a quieting effect on Grayson. The image of Becky as an entrepreneur gave him pause. "It's the principle of the thing."

"You attacked me for a principle? You better see a doctor." Dale pulled off his necktie and crumpled it into his pocket. He rubbed the shoulder he had landed on. "A doctor!" he repeated.

"Maybe we should call it a night," said Caleb, looking wearily from his roommate to his friend.

The taxi they flagged was an old blue gypsy cab with a springy back seat. Caleb sat between Grayson and Dale and they bounced along in silence.

18.

Strays and Accidentals

D<small>IANE</small> was waiting for him when Caleb arrived at the 72nd Street entrance to Central Park dressed in the khaki uniform he wore for bird-watching. She wore a red-and-white blouse striped like a beach umbrella, a red cotton skirt, and red sandals—not what he would describe as camouflage. He realized he had forgotten to tell her what to wear.

He took her hand and leaned toward her to kiss her on the cheek. Failing to commit himself to a side, he bumped her nose and kissed air.

"Is that some new way of kissing you invented? I find it very painful."

In the park they stopped to watch two boys in the playground kick and glide their silver swings to the fullest outstretched height. It was 9 a.m.

Caleb's 7 x 35-power binoculars bounced against his chest.

"Have you done this here before?"

"Birding? Once, in May. I came out before work one morning to see the warbler migration. I must have passed a dozen other men, all in suits, standing among the bushes."

They descended a flight of cement stairs and entered a dark underpass; pigeons overhead twirled down from the iron girders.

"Pigeons were one of Picasso's favorite subjects when he was a boy."

They circled the Bethesda Fountain and walked up the path under beech trees and sycamores, around the bank of the Boat Pond, over a bridge painted a dull rose color, and into the Ramble.

Caleb pointed out a redstart and identified the calls of a towhee, a wood pewee, and a purple finch. He explained what made identifying warblers such a good sport: the variety of species, their tiny size, shyness, and hyperactive behavior, all of which made them difficult to identify, particularly in the fall when the soft green plumage of many species was virtually identical. He let Diane look through the binoculars at a starling.

"I can't find it."

"Look at the bird without the glasses. Then, taking care to keep your hands steady, raise the glasses smoothly to your eyes."

"It works. Ooh! He's iridescent."

"It may be a *she*. The sexes are identical."

"That's what I like to hear."

"They're a European species. Eighty birds were released here in Central Park in the 1890s and now they're abundant from the East Coast to the Rockies."

Caleb asked to see the binoculars; he had heard a faint wheeze from the treetops and couldn't identify the call. Craning his neck, he scanned the branches. He took a few steps to one side; the muscles in the back of his neck pinched. The wheeze came again and he pinpointed the sound. There against the bark was a tiny brown-and-white bird, its bill curved like a thumbnail.

"Brown creeper," he said, releasing a breath of air. He pulled his field guide from his back pocket and flipped through it until he found the page: "A small inconspicuous bird with a soft voice."

"Sounds like you," said Diane.

"You mean inconspicuous?" He looked at her, puzzled.

"Your last name and your soft voice."

"I don't like the sound of that."

"You aren't what I would call noisy or boisterous."

"You think I'm passive."

She hesitated. "Reflective."

"Say what you mean."

"In a way you are passive. You don't seem to have deep commitments."

Caleb looped the binocular straps around his neck and looked up into the trees.

"I would understand you better, Caleb, if you were cynical. But I wouldn't like you as much. Talking to you sometimes, I get the feeling you're hiding from me. I thought maybe you'd had a traumatic childhood, but it certainly doesn't sound that way."

Caleb lowered the binoculars and looked at her shyly. "So you think I have some serious problems?" In a curious way it pleased him to hear this.

"A lack of commitment."

Could she possibly be inviting him to commit himself to her? Or did she mean professional commitments—that he should join a few associations? They walked along, side by side; Caleb scuffed at a pebble and it leapt up the path ahead of them.

"Can you be more specific?"

"To begin with, what are your values, Caleb? Values— just think about the word. A value is whatever makes something desirable or useful or excellent or important."

"Like money."

"Not that kind of value. The ethical kind."

"I'm open to suggestions."

"You want me to recommend some values for you? They're not like vitamins. They're not something you can prescribe."

"There's a very simple reason why I don't have enough values. I had no direct involvement with the Kennedy Years, Woodstock, the Vietnam War, and all that. I was too young. I was passed over. That's what I am—a member of the Passover Generation."

"Be serious. I think you have old-fashioned values and you just won't admit them because you don't want to be thought of as conventional."

"Maybe." He hadn't thought of that. He stopped and raised the binoculars to his face.

"You're looking in the wrong end," said Diane.

"I know that." He turned the binoculars on her; she shrank back twenty feet and held out a huge hand to him. Stay there, he thought, not wanting her to wound him in any of the numerous ways she had at her disposal. Why was it that in romance the loved one was always either too close or too far away? Why couldn't he get Diane to hold still in that middle distance?

He took her hand and they walked on. He found a blue-jay feather and showed her that it was not blue at all.

"Some feathers achieve their color through pigments and others through reflection and refraction of light."

"You mean they hide their true colors?"

"In a manner of speaking. A peacock's feather is actually brown."

"I'm keeping it." She put the feather in her pocketbook. "How well do you know the shore birds?"

"Once upon a time they were my strong suit. If you're on the beach, it helps to have a telescope because you can't get close to most shore birds. But that's where you see the strays and accidentals—birds that have been blown off course."

"Maybe I'll take a bird walk on the beach tomorrow."

"Which beach?"

"I'm going to the Hamptons for the day."

"Sounds like fun."

"With Gregory Miller."

He dropped her hand. "Mr. Miller?"

"He asked me a few weeks ago. I can't get out of it."
She picked up his hand and smoothed the fingers between

hers. "He's the client officer on the project I'm working on."

"He's the Managing Partner!"

"I'm aware of that."

"Isn't he married?"

"His wife left him. I think he's lonely." She looked at him and waited, but a dark mood had jumped and gagged him; he didn't say a word. Her expression was unmistakably one of disappointment. That meant she wanted him to stop her, to insist she stay in the city and spend the day with him, an unreasonable demand but exactly the sort she might want from him: an expression of commitment. He knew that now was the time to kiss her, but he felt he was being bullied into doing it, which made him all the more angry. He was in less than a kissing mood.

Instead he stood stupidly, his hands at his sides. She reached down and unfastened the straps of her red sandals, stepped out of them, and picked one up in each hand.

"Let's run," she said and broke from him, running on her toes up the hill to the top of the Ramble.

In a second he had shaken off his inexplicable, inexcusable lethargy and was racing desperately in pursuit. Hoping to cut her off as she came down the far side, he took a path that circled to the left. His sneakers thwacked on the hard-packed dirt and his toes stung; air scraped in and out of his lungs with each breath, a reminder of his deplorable physical condition. He pumped with his arms.

When he reached the back side of the hill, she was nowhere in sight. He thought at first she must be hiding, and he started up the hill, fully expecting her to jump out from behind a tree. Then he stopped and from the quality of the silence about him knew he was absolutely alone. He sprinted to the top and called her name. There was no reply. He walked briskly back down and started toward Fifth Avenue, but saw no sign of her ahead and finally decided she must have doubled back to wait for him by the bridge. He turned around again and jogged back through the Ramble. The bridge was empty; he had lost her.

He stopped twice on the way home to telephone her apartment, but got no answer. This worried him: Central Park was no place for a woman alone. The whole incident was very odd, and he didn't know whether to be offended or not.

Back at Yorkville Place, Robert was packed and ready to leave for the airport.

"I was just going to write you a note."

"You're leaving? But you just got here. We haven't *done* anything."

"I'm a madman. How could I abandon her when she is carrying my child? I must get back."

"Can't you stay at least until tomorrow? I have tonight free. I thought we could go see a play."

"No, Caleb. I've got responsibilities."

Caleb offered to ride with him to Kennedy. Since it was Saturday morning, they had little trouble finding a cab.

"I realized something about Dad last night while you were off at the fight. He thinks I'm deluded and I think he's deluded. The only difference is that he is obviously *happily* deluded. And you know something? I don't feel I've ever known him. I want my kid to know me."

Robert settled back in the seat, remarkably composed.

"Caleb, I just want to reiterate what I said about your life style here in New York. It's unhealthy. You should give some thought to moving to the country."

Caleb turned to face his brother. "I don't know quite how to put it, but I believe that I have to be a part of society, a member and a participant, in order to live a full life. Even if the society has its limitations."

"So you believe in the importance of the state—that makes you a bit of a socialist. They could use a few socialists on Wall Street."

"I'm not a socialist. I just feel this is where I belong."

At the airport, by the ticket counter, the brothers embraced for the first time in their lives. It made Caleb feel old.

"You know I'll need a Best Man."

"I would be honored," said Caleb.

"Me, too," said Robert, and he shuffled off into the terminal, a scraggly, bearded man in wrinkled clothing, a missionary bound for a tropical outpost.

Caleb was pleased with the role he had played in helping Robert conquer his marital misgivings. He had his bedroom and his privacy back and a trip to California to look forward to. Now if he could get through this assignment and straighten out this business with Diane, life would be on the upswing.

To save money Caleb took a subway back into the city. Before boarding he removed his wristwatch and signet ring and put them in his pocket as a precaution; he took a ten-dollar bill from his wallet and slid it into his shoe.

From the 57th Street station of the Train-to-the-Plane, Caleb walked east to the movie theaters at 59th Street and Third. He bought a Big Mac, hid it in his pocket until he was in the Coronet, and ate it quietly after the picture began.

There were times Caleb went to the movies on a friend's recommendation, or because the reviews were sensational. But recently he had begun to go with little regard for quality, and he went by himself. He paid his five dollars for a seat in the dark where he could let the images bombard him while he forgot who and where he was. Afternoon movies were the best because he lost all perception of time—he was hermetically sealed. A comfortable cinema like the Coronet was Caleb's idea of an urban isolation tank.

The film was a James Bond movie starring Roger Moore as 007. Caleb, who had seen all of the prior Bond movies, sat through it with an acute sense of déjà vu. After it was over he got up to use the john, decided to see the opening chase scene again, and ended up sitting through the whole picture and watching the opening sequence a third time. During those hours all thoughts of Diane and the Benefact Corp project were erased from his mind. His eyes were dry and sore when he boarded an empty Third Avenue bus for the trip uptown to his apartment.

In his refrigerator he found a case of Rolling Rock and a card signed, "Love, Robert." Caleb sat in the living room by the window, a cold beer bottle in one hand, his binoculars in the other. The sun dropped down like a beach ball behind the neighboring buildings, and Caleb felt disengaged from life, alone and afloat.

He peeked surreptitiously through the binoculars at the windows of empty apartments across Third Avenue, and at the young men and women emerging from Yorkville Place and the surrounding buildings in search of companionship or adventure. Caleb felt the magnetic tug of that night life so keenly he actually got up from the chair to change his clothes. What were the chances of tracking down Dale? He calculated the number of bars he could cover in an hour. Starting at Mumbles, a local hangout across the street, he could work his way south along Third, where the bars tended to be glittery and Waspy, stopping at Hoexter's, Jim McMullen's, and J.G. Melon's. And then he could cross to Second to check out the college crowd at the Mad Hatter, and zigzag over to First and York, where the bars were generally more Jappy or, in the case of Swells, full of MBAs. As a last resort he would check the Ravelled Sleave, the Sugar Mill, and Pedro's, collectively known as the Bermuda Triangle, which attracted a late-night crowd of heavy drinkers. But before he made it to his bedroom Caleb lost his motivation. For one thing, bar-hopping alone was awkward, people looked at you strangely. Then there was the money you spent and the liquor you drank. If he caroused until all hours of the morning, Sunday, which he should spend at the office, which he *must* spend at the office, would be wasted. He canceled his plans and sat down by the window to drink another beer.

19.

Sabbath

T H E sections of the Sunday *Times* were spread out at Caleb's feet and he was just getting to work on it, leafing through the Travel section, scrutinizing ads of bikini-clad bathers on Jamaican beaches and moored sloops in Caribbean coves, when Bob Sparrow telephoned to invite him out to brunch. Caleb accepted the invitation out of a sense of duty. He had certainly seen enough of his father over the past week, and he was beginning to look forward to Gretchen's return from Switzerland, if just to take his father off his hands.

He knew, without asking, where to meet him. Sunday for Bob and Gretchen Sparrow was as regimented as the rest of the week. When they were in New York for a weekend (which was rare in the summer) they ate Sunday brunch at a restaurant a block from their building. The owner was a friend and always reserved the same corner table for them. Bob Sparrow's closest associates—his Chief Operating Officer at Olympus Brands, his lawyer, and his financial advisor—knew where he brunched and that they could always reach him there by phone.

The maitre d' led Caleb to the table and presented him to his father as though he were one of the specials of the day.

"Get Caleb a drink," said Bob Sparrow, rising with a smile to shake Caleb's hand.

"Ginger ale. I'm on my way to the office."

Bob Sparrow nodded approvingly; they took their seats.

"I had a call from your roommate yesterday."

"Dale?"

"I thought he was calling to thank me for our outing— and he did—but can you guess his real reason for calling?"

"I can't." There could be any number of heinous reasons.

"He asked me to switch banks. He wants to manage my account."

"Oh, I'm sorry. How embarrassing."

"Well, exactly. Nevertheless, I like that young man. With that kind of aggressiveness he'll do well."

"They both enjoyed the fight."

"What did you do afterwards?"

"Oh, we just went to a little bar Dale goes to . . . and talked about college."

"A little reminiscing, is that it?"

"College seems like ages ago."

"I liked your friends, Caleb. And you can take a man's measure by looking at his friends."

"Thank you."

"I can't help but think how different you and your brother are."

Could he have heard about Robert's wedding plans?

"What's wrong with Robert?"

"It's not that there's so much wrong with the boy. He's got wonderful qualities. But we have to face the facts. He is not going to amount to much. Your stepmother describes him as the kind of person who always makes people uncomfortable at cocktail parties."

What about her!

"You're exaggerating, Dad."

Bob Sparrow looked up from the menu. "Caleb, there are certain mistakes you can make in life from which you never recover."

Caleb was sure he had heard that line before, and this time it rankled him.

"—Robert has made his share and more."

"What exactly do you expect us to be, Dad? Don't we get any credit for being normal, decent people?"

"I don't follow," said Bob Sparrow.

"Don't you see? Robert and I are not super achievers. And neither of us has any great desire to be a super achiever. Do I look to you like a future CEO? You know that's ridiculous!"

Caleb, fully expecting to be interrupted and reprimanded for his outburst, proceeded to tell his father that he would much rather be his friend and son than one more of his trophies.

Bob Sparrow winced at the mention of trophies. "All right, Caleb. I see what you're saying. You're trying to be realistic in your expectations. That's a mature approach. But I've been in this business for twenty-eight years. I think I know what works."

Caleb wasn't sure if his father meant by "this business" the business world or the business of being a father. There had never been a clear distinction.

"No matter what your talents, what your position in the world, never admit your weaknesses—not to your friends, not to your rivals. It will cost you their respect."

Caleb felt his jaw drop. His father had not heard a word he had said, not really. Caleb started to speak and caught himself: did it matter if his father understood? He decided it was unrealistic to insist on absolute candor when his father clung to a myopic outlook on life in which appearances, self-control, and confidence were the key indices of character. Why not let him believe he had a son of professional promise? It seemed to give him a satisfaction as keen as any from his work. Caleb suddenly felt sorry for his father, who seemed trapped in a coldly ordered world sealed off from life in the streets, halls, and mailrooms. And so he dropped the subject of his future and asked his father for advice on how to conduct himself during the Benefact presentation.

Bob Sparrow recommended Caleb modulate his voice tone.

"You tend to talk in a monotone. Also, don't volunteer

a lot of extraneous information. Stick to the report and the subject at hand."

His father was pleased to be able to offer these suggestions, and before the meal was over Caleb reaffirmed that strange, even improbable friendship he and his father had, the seemingly accidental fact that they liked each other.

It was not unusual for a quarter of the professional staff to show up at H&L at some point on Sunday to attend to pressing assignments, to catch up on some analysis, or to monitor the printing of a report as it went through Report Production, which more often than not was open on Sunday. Some consultants showed up simply by force of habit; for them the office was the place they felt most at home, and to miss a Sunday afternoon was to miss a family gathering. There was a distinct and festive air to H&L on such afternoons. The lounge was noisy and crowded.

When Caleb arrived, two principals were distributing jelly doughnuts to the assembled company. Caleb had too much work to do to waste time talking—he went directly to his desk. Pike had come by and left a dead cigar butt and a sour smoke smell. No sign of Grayson.

Caleb sat at his desk in his green alcove and puttered. He straightened the contents of every drawer, grouping the paper clips and the pencils and the rubber bands. The Sunday *Times* had carried an article on the plight of the aviation industry. This he filed in a Pendaflex folder marked "B.C. Misc." in the cabinet beside his desk. He filled out his Time and Expense Report, billing the allowable forty hours to Benefact Corp. His expenses that week were limited to his taxi fare home on Monday night, which he estimated and entered as $4.50. It was standard practice to write off your travel expenses if you stayed at the office past seven. He readdressed two brown interoffice envelopes—one to Jim Pike and one to the Accounting Office—folded a carbon of the T&E into each, and kept the original for his own records. When he finally looked at the Benefact Corp working papers, his life was in order. Printing neatly, he wrote a title on each exhibit.

The work went well for half an hour or so. He proceeded at a steady clip, humming softly to himself. But then he daydreamed he was on the beach with Diane, spreading suntan lotion over her back. He pictured his hands gliding over her bony shoulderblades the way they had during the back rub on Thursday night. His hands were transposed with a second pair of hands and then his disappeared altogether. The pair that remained, hairy and obscene, belonged to Gregory Miller, Managing Partner. Caleb broke the point of his pencil on the spread sheet. Less than a minute later he was in Diane's office with the door closed, searching for some memento, some trace of her he could have for his own. The drawers to her desk were locked. He picked up her *World Almanac* and shook it open, expecting something—a snapshot, a note—to fall out. Her wastebasket was, of course, empty. He sniffed her desk, smelled nothing. In fact, there was no trace of her whatsoever, and, looking around, he realized the bare-walled room could have been anyone's office. He rocked back in her swivel chair and put a hand to his heart.

"Careful, Caleb. You'll have a heart attack," he said out loud in a flat voice he did not recognize as his own.

"Think what you're doing," the voice continued. What *was* he doing, other than making a complete idiot of himself? he wondered. "She's not here," he said next, feigning a rational pretense for his conduct. "She's definitely not here." He replaced the *World Almanac*.

To Caleb's great relief, four of the companies in the comparative sample had no stock-option plan; this saved him hours of work. He noticed that most of the proxy statements listed the major perquisites available to the top corporation officers. Although he realized he was making work for himself when he could least afford to, he decided to draw up an exhibit showing which perquisites were most prevalent. Perquisites, after all, were a form of compensation. The exhibit took him an hour and a half. He was pleased with it: it was the sort of work Pike and Beauregard could point to as showing initiative.

He ate a yogurt at his desk for dinner and crunched numbers until midnight.

20.

Caleb's Blue Period

A gray limousine pulled up to the curb in front of the Reeves Building the next morning as Caleb, arriving for work, stood on the south side of 47th Street waiting for the light to change. The chauffeur ran around the long nose of the car and opened the passenger door. Out stepped Gregory Miller, who turned and offered his hand to a companion. And there was Diane, sunburned, smiling. Caleb whirled around to avoid being seen.

Grayson met him at the door of the researchers' room, nervously jiggling the change in his pocket. "I've got to talk to you, Caleb."

"Fine," said Caleb, in no mood to talk to anyone. He followed Grayson to his desk. The can of Bosco was out.

"Yesterday I broke up with Jamie."

"You did?"

"I thought you should know because you're a friend of ours and one of the few people who know about us. You see, after my promotion I started thinking about our relationship and what would happen if the secret got out, and I realized I had to do something." Grayson shook the change. "Finally I decided I just couldn't risk it any more. People will be watching me and judging every aspect of my performance. I told her she had to quit and try to get that job at Macy's or we had to break up. Well, she won't quit."

"It all seems so sudden."

"I suppose it is. Actually, I've had reservations for some time. Look at the matter long-term. I can't marry her."

"Because she's a secretary?"

"It's not just that. It's how she presents herself. She's not dignified enough."

Caleb said he was sorry.

"I knew you would understand."

Caleb retreated to his desk, not at all sure he did understand. Grayson, he decided, was a snob. Poor Jamie. Her problems made his look small. Maybe now was to time to buy her flowers. Or would that make her feel worse? She was not at her desk. Gloria, the secretary who sat next to her, hadn't seen her.

Ten minutes later Caleb walked through the reception area, took a left under the stairs, and headed straight for Diane's office. He knocked on her door; no answer. She had gone for coffee. Today her presence was everywhere: a suitcase stood against the wall, her blue blazer hung on the back of her chair, the contents of her pocketbook—

the rich accouterments of her life—were strewn over the top of her desk. The blue-jay feather was there, and a small bottle filled with tiny orange pills. There was no prescription on the bottle. What was she taking medication for? Was she ill?

He wrote a note on a piece of scrap paper: "How about lunch?—C."

The first call that morning was from his mother. She began by apologizing for not reaching him on his birthday. She said she had tried him at home but that there had been no answer.

"What do you suppose I just heard?" she said.

"Tell me."

"Your brother, Robert, is to be married!"

"Yes, I know."

"And you kept it a secret?"

"He asked me to."

"Rupert and I are very encouraged. I'm flying out on Saturday to help with the arrangements."

"So soon? I thought the wedding was in August."

"There's tons to do. I've spoken to the bride's mother. Where do you suppose she lives? Locust Valley!"

"Long Island?" The significance of this fact escaped him. "Will it be a big ceremony?"

"Three hundred guests. However, it's a joint ceremony."

"What do you mean 'joint,' Mom?"

"Six couples."

"Six?"

"Now, Caleb, don't say anything. I have a good feeling about this."

"I'm not *saying* a thing. What has he told you about her?"

"He said that she's lovely and that she's the congregation's nutritionist and that she's Caucasian—thank God."

She was prepared to forgive Robert everything if he married, which she would interpret as a concession to her values. Robert and she would patch up their differences— Caleb could see it coming. And these developments, these pending mergers, weren't such a bad thing. Caleb was acutely aware of how little he had to report that would be meaningful to his mother, and hoped she would not ask how he was or what was new. But when, in her excitement, she didn't, concluding with a brief description of her travel plans—Northwest Orient, a DC-10, non-stop—he hung up wishing that she had.

At 11:30 Caleb finished running the numbers for Pike's relative-performance compensation plan. He gathered the papers into a stack and carried them to Pike's office. The principal switched the receiver of the phone from his left to his right hand and motioned Caleb into the seat beside his desk. He stared intently at the wall in front of him, nodded once, said, "Do that," and hung up.

"In the last month I've made five grand on the stock of a company which manufactures wheelchairs. I'm exploiting demographics." He scratched behind one ear. "Makes up for that damn chinchilla farm Beauregard had me invest in. What have you got?"

Caleb handed him the spread sheets. Pike leafed through the pile once quickly to see what was there and a second time to read the numbers, tracing the columns with his index finger. Caleb twisted his neck to follow Pike's progress; every pause of that index finger could mean an error. Caleb silently urged it on.

"Can we show this graphically?" Pike asked, pointing to a sheet dense with numbers. "And we definitely need a flow chart to explain the steps of the plan. Otherwise looks fine. I like the perquisites exhibit. Look at *this* guy. He gets a car, first-class air travel, dining and country club membership, annual medical exam, a hundred percent medical and dental reimbursement, financial/tax counseling, and a low-interest loan. What does that leave? He has no expenses!"

"Something to look forward to," said Caleb.

"Who is it? Do you remember?"

"Executive E? That's Ransome."

"Figures. Put him at the bottom and underline him."

"Do you think Ransome is in it just for the money?"

"There is that possibility," said Pike.

"Do you think he's sincere?"

"In his own way."

"What about in our way? How can we begin to set compensation levels if we don't know the truth?"

"Caleb, this is not a religion class. As far as I'm concerned, there's only one thing that matters and that's the compensation plan. I want *it* to be perfect. Now go back and check your numbers. All of them. I don't care if it takes all night."

Jamie had not appeared by the time Caleb left for lunch and he doubted now that she would be in that day.

He met Diane in the reception area. Her sunburn began at her forehead, deepened over her cheeks and nose, and was its deepest red at her throat just where it disappeared into her blouse. He thought it very becoming, but didn't say so.

"Hurt much?"

"I burned my ass."

The implications of that remark left Caleb speechless. A security guard held the door for them; they walked out to the elevators.

"I feel like oysters," she said, licking her lips suggestively. "They're a low-calorie aphrodisiac."

"How can you be worried about getting fat?" he said grumpily.

"I guess I'm not," she conceded. "It's the aphrodisiac I was thinking about."

She meant the aphrodisiac to be for him. How could she talk like that after betraying him?

"Say something, Caleb."

"Why did you run away from me in Central Park?"

"Oh, that. I started running and it felt so good I couldn't stop. I'm sorry. I didn't do it deliberately. I felt badly when I realized I'd lost you."

He wasn't going to whine about it. Not about that or anything else: he would be calm and lucid. Besides, what bothered him more was this business with Miller and the pills. The thought flashed across his mind that the pills might have a contraceptive function. He had the forbearance not to mention either subject until they were seated in the cavernous Oyster Bar and Restaurant in Grand

Central. She talked vaguely about her day on the beach while Caleb tried to get a waitress's attention. When one finally passed their table carrying two glasses of water, Caleb touched her arm.

"Can't you see I'm busy?" she snapped.

"Don't rush her," said Diane.

"I'm hardly rushing her. We've been sitting here for at least ten minutes."

"Caleb, you're so peevish. Where is the old Caleb, the funny, shy Caleb I met a week ago?"

"I'm tired of people telling me how I should behave. So what if I am peevish?"

"This is not going well," said Diane to the ceiling.

Caleb gave her a hard look. "What do you care? I saw you arrive for work this morning. I think you're probably wasting your time with me."

"What do I care?" She sat back and squinted at him, her head tipped to one side. "You want to know what I care about? I care about lonely, middle-aged men who miss their wives, *and* I care about peevish bird-watchers who can't express themselves emotionally. I care. That's all I do is care. But I'll tell you one thing, I'm sick and tired of doing *all* the caring."

"You said you were going to the Hamptons for the day."

"And he invited me to spend the night."

"Did you sleep with him?"

"Caleb, so help me. I'll slap you, too."

"Answer the question."

She blushed through her sunburn.

"He kissed me, damn you. And it was nice. It's more

than you've ever done." She rose and reached for her pocketbook.

He leaned over and seized her thin wrists. "Sit down!" he said coolly, pulling on her.

She shook loose. "How dare you!"

"There is something I've got to talk to you about."

"I can see I was wrong about you," she said.

"And I about you. That's what I want to talk about."

She rose and swung her pocketbook strap over her shoulder. "I don't need you." She looked glorious, furious.

"What do you want?" asked the waitress, attentive now that a table was at stake.

"Trust!" said Diane, raging. "You have spoiled something special!"

"Me?" said the waitress, meekly.

Before Caleb could rise to stop her, Diane, for a second time, had run out on him. He sat examining his paper place mat. He scratched his cheek, touched his napkin to his mouth, took a sip of water, rubbed his eyes. The restaurant seemed terribly crowded and noisy. He ordered a bowl of oyster stew and ate it, brooding, before returning to the office.

His duties for the remainder of the day were to come up with a few handsome exhibits for the compensation plan and to double-check his arithmetic. He performed both without joy. A headache clamped onto his forehead and made his eyes water. He asked Gloria to type some spread sheets for him. She read some numbers wrong and he found himself about to shout at her; he made himself hold his tongue and turn away.

The ironic part about his argument with Diane was that he knew if he cared any less about her he would have no trouble apologizing. Of course, his willfulness about not apologizing was a more honest response because he *was* willful, and she should know that about him. If he was behaving selfishly it was because she contradicted him constantly; she'd fallen asleep during his back rub; and twice she had ditched him in the middle of a date. He had a right to be mad at her.

At home that night, lying in bed, he found a little corner for her in his thoughts, a nook where he could tuck her and for a time she would stay. He did this by reminding himself of her last words and convincing himself that she couldn't love him. And he argued with himself that he had no time for her, particularly now as the Benefact Corp presentation approached. She could ruin his concentration and mar his performance. And this business with Miller— didn't that make her an opportunist? A man in his position would be very helpful to her career development. Caleb recalled his interview with the Managing Partner and, rolling over, thrashed his pillow. In this way he kept thoughts of her at bay. It was only when he recalled the pills that she escaped her nook, and he asked himself how he could be so concerned with his own happiness when the important thing, if she was sick, was to do what he could to help her.

Caleb awoke in the dark to whispers and was afraid. Burglars! He opened his eyes a fraction, dreading a knife in the chest at any moment. His door was open and two shapes stood by his bureau. He could not make out what they were doing. His wallet was on the bureau top—they would find that. His jewelry would be safe; he had hidden his tie clips, studs, cufflinks, and a scratched Timex in the spider plant. Caleb's heart was thumping so hard he was sure they would hear it. Robert was right: the city was no place to live; not just unhealthy—dangerous. If only there had been just one burglar; Caleb might have leaped out of bed and grappled with him. In his mind he located objects in the room which could be used as weapons. These included Samuelson's *Economics*, his night table, a pair of scissors in his desk drawer, his squash racquet in his closet. The closet! The two figures were creeping across the room to the closet at the foot of his bed. Caleb seethed at the injustice of it; they were going to plunder his wardrobe.

The two figures crouched at the foot of the bed. My shoes, thought Caleb, they want my shoes!

More whispers.

"Give me a hand with this. Actually, it takes two hands."

"Braggart. . . . Putty."

"It's the suspense. Pull here."

Caleb stiffened. That reference to putty. Were they going to dynamite his room? Did they think there was a safe?

"Better?"

"Mmm."

"Get it in."

One was a woman! She had a softer voice. Squinting through his eyelashes, Caleb could just make out the silhouette of her head and hair.

Instead of crawling into the closet, the male burglar seemed to climb on the other's back. Caleb had a jarring thought followed by sickening apprehension.

"I hope he's up for this."

"That's my department."

Piggyback, the two intruders began to crawl onto Caleb's bed.

"Ahhh!" yelled Caleb when a hand touched his leg, instantly yanking himself up to a sitting position and lunging for the light switch. The three of them were caught and blinded in the brilliant light: Caleb with a hand to his thumping chest, and his intruders—stark naked!— Dale and a frizzy-haired, big-breasted woman Caleb had never laid eyes on before. Dale pressed up to his playmate's rear end, his hands on her hips. He smiled serenely at Caleb.

"How about it, Caleb? Interested in a ménage à trois?"

Caleb made three short, choking coughs of astonishment and failed to speak.

"Hit the lights," the woman ordered, crawling toward him on her elbows, pendulous breasts swinging. She reached out a claw and snagged Caleb by the waistband of his jockey shorts.

"Ahhh!" yelled Caleb. He scrambled out of bed, freeing himself in the process—the elastic snapped painfully. He ducked into the bathroom and locked the door and sat on the toilet seat.

"I don't believe this."

He got up and opened the bathroom door a crack.

"Dale, get that woman out of my bed! Get her out of my

217

room or I swear I'll break the lease tomorrow. You've gone too far."

He listened for their voices.

"That's it, honey," said Dale. "The fun's over. He didn't take the bait. Maybe another time."

"'What a square!'"

21.

Diane's Deficit

J AMIE, her hair cut short and permed, sat typing at her desk looking pretty and purposeful, a pencil in her teeth. She removed it to say good morning. Caleb complimented her on her new haircut.

"I needed a new look to go with my new style. Does it say 'Who gives a damn?' to you?"

"I'm sorry about you and Grayson."

"Those are the politics of romance for you. I'm transferring to the twenty-sixth floor. I can't sit here broken-hearted and watch that executive-on-training-wheels come and go all day long. Can you imagine me taking messages from his next girlfriend?"

He promised to visit her.

"Say, I hear *your* friend took a leave of absence."

That was how he first heard about Diane. At his desk Pridgeon, who had been lying in wait for him, provided the details.

"I heard your friend cracked."

"Cracked what?"

Pridgeon looked at him uncertainly. "Oh, boy, wait until you hear. This morning Liz, your friend's secretary, comes in early and hears this banging on the door. She opens it and out comes Diane, disheveled, babbling about being locked in her office all night and having to catch a plane to Salt Lake City. Thing is, the door locks, but only from the inside. And she had red Magic Marker scribbled on her face and arms. You should see her office walls."

Caleb pushed Pridgeon out of his way.

"She lost her marbles, all right," Pridgeon called after him.

On the wall facing her desk Caleb saw she had drawn a giant bouquet of long-stemmed roses. She had titled the work "Flowers for Diane" and signed and dated it in the lower righthand corner. Another wall was covered with columns, scribbled theorems, and graphs with looping parabolas. Two men from maintenance with paint and brushes were in the room spreading drop cloths over the floor.

Liz, at Caleb's side, dabbed her eyes with Kleenex.

"She asked me if I had seen her parachute. I said, 'You mean your pocketbook?' She said, 'No, no'—in this sleepy voice. I asked her if she wanted a cup of coffee, and she said, 'Water, please.' So I ran down the hall and told Michelle in Personnel to get help. It was Michelle who called Bellevue. I ran back with a cup of water, but she hadn't moved. The way she took the cup . . . both hands, like a little girl! 'You're nice,' she said. She had no idea who I was. I told her she was nice, too, and that's when I started to cry. She told me everything would be okay, and she hugged me, and I hugged her. When Michelle came with the paramedics, she said, 'I was on my way to Salt Lake City. I'm glad you stopped me. I have work to do. I can't possibly leave.' She was so matter-of-fact. And when one of the attendants helped her into her blazer, she asked him if he wanted to marry her."

"Did anyone call her parents?" asked Caleb.

"Michelle. I was too upset."

Back at his desk Caleb tried to stay calm. Then he exploded from his chair, ripping the green computer paper off all the walls and sweeping his telephone onto the floor.

Grayson made him sit down again and take deep breaths, bent over with his chin at his knees. The phone on the floor began to beep frantically. Grayson picked it up and collected the sheets of computer paper. With his arm around Caleb's shoulder, he walked with him to the lounge, where he mixed him a cup of Bosco.

"How are you feeling?" asked Pike, who had come by Caleb's desk after hearing the news.

"Awful." The word did no justice to the misery he felt. "It's my fault. I had a fight with her yesterday."

"Don't be an idiot. They found a hundred tabs of uppers in her pocketbook. She's a speed freak. That's what did it to her. I'm willing to bet that if she hadn't met a nice guy like you she would have flipped out ages ago."

"I just started dating her last week."

"Oh." Pike cleared his throat. "Still. I bet you're one of the better things that have happened to her. A woman like that in this business is bound to have a rough time. After all, men were here first."

"What difference does it make who was here first?"

"Caleb, you don't blame me for what happened, do you?"

"No. I'm more to blame than anybody. I'm such a jerk sometimes."

"Don't talk like that—you're my prize research analyst. Together we have written a masterpiece in the field of executive compensation. Tell you what. Proof the text pages I wrote last night. That will take your mind off what happened, and then together we can deliver this epic to Report Production. Looks a lot better in here without all that paper on the wall."

Pike was right: to do something, anything, helped. At four, the two of them delivered the report to RP for final revisions and printing. They stood in Linda's office before surrendering it. Pike planted noisy kisses on the title page, while she tried to grab it away, insisting she had a backlog and a headache and no time for his games.

Caleb left work early and went directly to Bellevue. Although it was visiting hours, he was not allowed to see Diane. He was told she had been given a sedative and was sleeping peacefully. Her parents would be staying at the Plaza.

At home Dale had left all the lights on and the refrigerator door open. The Rolling Rock was warm; Caleb drank seven bottles before he was drunk. For the first time he smelled the rank odor of carrion which Robert had described. Perhaps someone had died in the apartment below. Caleb, collapsing on his bed with a grunt, didn't much care.

BC

H E ran his tongue over his mossy teeth when he awoke with a headache the next morning; he sat up and was wrenched by a sneeze. In his belly a gyroscope wobbled on a string, maintaining a tenuous equilibrium. He asked himself if he was unhappy and realized the question no longer applied. When he thought of Diane, a wave of guilt and worry broke over him.

Without rushing, his footfalls soft, he made his way to the bathroom and doctored himself by gulping down a bitter solution of aspirin dissolved in tap water. Barefoot before his closet, squinting, he tried to guess what the top officers of Benefact Corp wore to their Board meetings. Manufacturing was no white-shoe industry. Executives with engineering backgrounds would favor gray glen-plaids resembling graph paper; the rest, solid-color poplins. He decided on the olive-green poplin with black buttons—his favorite suit. He scooped a token's worth of bureau-top coins into his palm and, noticing that a light rain was falling from the slate ceiling of sky, took along the stiff raincoat his father had given him.

He was short of breath when he reached the office, and his heart was pounding. He drew in successive lungfuls of the firm's dry, metallic air, expecting the headache to return at any moment.

His reports sat in a stack of twelve on the table just inside the door of Report Production; beside them, the cardboard box of transparencies. He raised the stack and held it like a chalice, his relief magnificent.

Clear plastic cover, gray frontispiece, and matching tabs —each report had the sweet mulch-and-iodine smell of fresh paper and ink. He flipped through the copies one at a time to ensure they were complete and in order; then, with the stack cradled in his arms, edging sideways through doors, he navigated the halls, descended the stairs, and elbowed open the door to Beauregard's office.

The partner yawned, still puffy-looking from sleep. Pike had used a hair tonic, so that his slicked-back hair had a glaze. His eyes were bright and alert. They exchanged good mornings. Caleb handed them each a copy of the report, and for the next fifteen minutes they checked for typographical errors, reviewed Pike's compensation plan, and discussed the presentation.

Caleb sat on the windowsill where Pike had sat the day Caleb was offered a job. He scratched the back of his hand and gently tapped his pencil in his palm.

"Looks fine," said Beauregard. "Very thorough. Shows some imagination, and I think they'll like that."

"State-of-the-art compensation work," said Pike.

"You put a lot of yourself into this report, Jim. I can see that."

"Caleb, too."

"I'm not forgetting Caleb."

Hardly a compliment, thought Caleb. And no mention of his perquisites exhibit. It didn't much matter. Pike would write the job-end appraisal, just as he handled most of the partner's client-related mail, and Pike would be sure to say what needed to be said. The important thing now was the presentation. If that was a big success, Caleb stood a shot at a promotion; at the very least he would become what was termed "researcher of choice" on strategy and human-resource-related assignments, which meant greater responsibility, more autonomy, and a raise.

A Benefact proxy statement lay on Beauregard's desk, open to the page containing photographs and short biographies of the Board members. Seven of the twelve Board members were on the Executive Committee. Pike, who had spoken to Fowler, the COO, that morning, said only six would make the meeting—three insiders and three outsiders. A week before, Caleb had Xeroxed the *Who's Who* entry of each Committee member; Beauregard wanted to know what clubs they belonged to, where they lived, their wives' maiden names, and if they had children. This gave him ammunition for small talk. The inside directors were George Appleton, the founder and Chairman of Benefact Corp, eighty; Albert Fowler, the COO and Treasurer, fifty-nine; and Ransome. The outside directors were Hubert Blair, Managing Partner of Hill & Dale, the public-relations firm, fifty-three; Lawrence Kimberly, Senior Partner, Ropes & Chaynes, attorneys at law, fifty-eight; and Stuart Bowles, Distinguished Professor of Psychology, Columbia University, retired, sixty-seven. Pike and Caleb had interviewed Ransome. Beauregard had interviewed Fowler. No one had met Appleton or the outsiders.

"I predict," said Pike, "that Ransome will abstain from the discussion of his own compensation. Appleton and Blair will go with the flow. Fowler is in Ransome's corner. So if we have to sell this thing, let's sell it to Kimberly and Bowles—they're rumored to be the two sharpest minds on the Board and the ones most capable of swaying Appleton and Blair."

"Bowles is the one I worry about," said Beauregard. "Academics think they represent a higher authority. They talk too much and have little appreciation for the rules of parliamentary procedure."

Beauregard decided he would deliver the introduction, then turn the presentation over to Jim. He said he would interject where he saw fit. Pike said that sounded fine; he and Caleb exchanged amused looks.

"Caleb," continued Beauregard, "don't speak unless spoken to, and only then if it pertains to our analysis or methodology."

They agreed to reconvene in half an hour. A cab would be waiting.

Back at his desk Caleb boxed the reports and fastened the lid shut with adhesive tape, running the roll around and around the box until, stopping, he realized how much he had done and tried to unwind it. He collected the spread sheets and every scrap of paper with jotted notes or numbers and stuffed them into his briefcase. In front of the men's-room mirror he wet and combed his hair, pinched his cheek to bring reluctant blood to his face, and slipped on the Brooks Brothers raincoat. His hands didn't shake but he seemed to watch himself from afar.

Forty-five minutes later the three H&L executives, surrounded by twelve leather club chairs—each with a standing lamp and mahogany side table—huddled in the antechamber of the Benefact Corp boardroom awaiting a signal that the Executive Committee was ready to receive them. Through the windows Caleb could see blocks of buildings up the glistening wet Avenue of the Americas— the palaces of the oil and entertainment industries where he had been interviewed seven months before. As quietly as possible Caleb tore open the box which held the reports; the cardboard made a loud ripping sound.

The oak door to the boardroom opened and out walked Appleton, the Chairman, a tall, wobbly man in a loose, dark suit which must have fit once but was now floppy-shouldered, long in the arms, and baggy in the crotch. His gait was an irregular and swivel-hipped shuffle assisted by a black cane which Caleb mistook for an iron poker. He looked much older than his annual-report photo, his thick white hair yellowed in spots. He stabbed the carpet with his cane and muttered the word "Damn" as though he had just missed skewering some vermin.

After serving in the Air Force during World War I, he had built the company from scratch, working out of his basement in the early years. He had survived a fabled smear campaign and efforts to deny him credit, surpassing his competitors in ten years, outliving them in twenty.

"Arthritis," said Appleton. "This weather doesn't help a bit."

"Miserable day," said Beauregard, delighted Appleton himself had come out to greet them. "I'd like you to meet Jim Pike and Caleb Sparrow."

There was plenty of strength left in Appleton's grip; when they shook hands, Caleb's knuckles cracked.

"Caleb is Bob Sparrow's boy. Bob Sparrow of Olympus Brands."

Appleton screwed his watery, sunken eyes into focus; Caleb wondered if he had been drinking.

"Good for you, boy—working for H&L. Bet your dad is pleased."

"Dad is pleased," said Beauregard.

"Yes," said Caleb.

Appleton pointed toward the boardroom with his cane. "Let's not keep the gang waiting. We've got work to do. Caleb, come see my boardroom."

Following Appleton, Caleb could not ignore the growing conviction that he had just witnessed the major reason Beauregard had brought him along, in fact, hired him in the first place: to show off H&L's connections and make explicit the consanguinity among businessmen. Caleb might have to defend a few numbers or the choice of companies in the comparative sample, but that in itself was insufficient reason for his presence. But as the son of a Chief Executive and a young man in Beauregard's employ, he was proof that the old-boy network endured.

Painted on the concave ceiling of the Benefact Corp boardroom was a scene of tumbling cumulus clouds in an empty aqua-blue sky. No prophets, no angels, no gigantic deity stretching to create an unblemished Adam, just an empty, birdless, partly cloudy sky. The paneled black oak walls of the boardroom had the sealed feeling of a vault. The oval table was of matching oak and varnished so it reflected the clouds overhead. A thick central stem fastened it to the floor and gave it the look of a giant toadstool.

The H&L project team was shown to seats on one side of the table. Before each of the six men of the Executive Committee was a plate, a yellow legal pad, a brand-new pencil with an impress of the BC logo, and a set of silver salt and pepper shakers in the shape of the Penguin 10 turbo fan jet—a corporate gift. Breakfast was in progress. The Committee men were eating a watery mix of scrambled eggs and black olives. All but one were dressed in solid-color poplins, just as Caleb had expected. They were men Grayson had once described as "lifers." Caleb had studied the proxy statement and could identify them without difficulty.

Appleton's seat was at the head of the table. On his right, Ransome, the Sir Lancelot of Benefact Corp, sat immobile—his breakfast plate clean. With each long, steady breath he seemed to suck up much of the room's still air. The knot of his necktie looked flimsy against his throat.

On Appleton's left sat Fowler, the Chief Operating Officer and Treasurer of the company, crew-cut, his up-turned, wide-nostril nose a suitable tool for rutting among numbers. Pike had described his mind as a hornet's nest of intelligence. Prices and the cost-of-goods-sold were the central preoccupations of his life.

Beside Fowler sat Lawrence Kimberly, the lawyer— attractive, well groomed. His Ivy League credentials brought cachet to the Benefact Board, a little tradition and breeding to what was in Beauregard's opinion a barbarous industry. A pleasant man to watch and listen to, a thrush in the woods.

Hubert Blair of Hill & Dale, the public-relations firm, intercepted Appleton on his way back to his seat. He talked out of the side of his mouth; he was a back-slapper. His conversation with Appleton had something to do with the greens at Augusta.

At the end of the row, in a seat opposite Caleb, sat the Board's academic, Stuart Bowles. He was bent over his plate intent on his eggs, shielding them with his elbows. He ignored Blair, who, returning to his seat, gave him a wink.

A smocked waitress began to clear plates. With Appleton seated and shuffling papers in his lap, Pike broke off his conversation with Beauregard and advised Caleb to distribute the reports. Caleb removed nine copies from the box, stacked three in front of Pike, and began to circle the table.

"More coffee," said Bowles, looking up at Caleb.

"I don't work here," said Caleb, embarrassed. "I'm from H&L."

Kimberly, who had witnessed the exchange, stood up and formally shook Caleb's hand. Fowler and Ransome said, "Thanks." Appleton had spread the *Wall Street*

Journal like a napkin in his lap, open to the New York Stock Exchange composite transactions.

"Good boy," he said when Caleb handed him a copy of the report. Gin breath.

To men who were used to deciding whether or not to sell jet engines to the Arabs, when to negotiate with the AFL-CIO, how to court the Administration's favor and win contracts from the Pentagon, a compensation study would be a trifle. The study, Caleb realized as he returned to his seat, would hold only the peripheral interest of half-time entertainment at a football game.

Pike adjusted the aim of the projector, then motioned to Ransome that he was ready. Ransome nodded to Appleton, and the Chairman, in a slow, measured, almost disinterested voice, introduced Beauregard and the project team from Hooker & Lyman. Beauregard cleared his throat. Leaning forward, he explained the purpose of the study and the approach the team had chosen to follow. The project had been interesting and, from H&L's perspective, immensely satisfying. The work was finished on schedule, under budget, and some of the compensation work they were about to see was state-of-the-art. Beauregard turned the meeting over to Pike and, with evident relief, rolled back into his chair.

Pike placed the first transparency in the projector.

"The prevailing philosophy in executive compensation today is that to effectively attract, motivate, and retain senior management talent, a company's compensation system must be coordinated with the company's strategic plan. What we are proposing here is a performance-sensitive compensation arrangement driven by the key indices of your company's growth and efficiency—namely, earnings per share and return on equity. . . ."

What most impressed Caleb about Pike's oratory was the fluidity of his speech. He had none of the mechanical qualities of a course-taught public speaker. His voice had range and timbre. Pike covered the report page by page, slide by slide. The Executive Committee followed the presentation attentively. Nobody interrupted. In fact, they betrayed no reaction whatsoever, which seemed to make Beauregard uneasy. When the bar chart showing Ransome's salary relative to other CEOs in the industry appeared on the screen, a skyscraper among town houses, there was a small commotion of mutters and whispers. Ransome pushed back his chair and rose from the table. Beauregard sat up straight.

Ransome apologized for interrupting the presentation. "Jim, you may leave that chart up. That's what we're here to see."

He strode back and forth behind the chairs of his fellow Committee members; it had a peculiar effect on them: they focused their attention on the pads and pencils before them.

"We are discussing my compensation: do I deserve what I get and should I get more?"

Ransome said he didn't feel he should be present while they made their decision, but before he left the room he wanted to say a few things for the record.

He spoke extemporaneously of his childhood ambition to be a test pilot and of the sad reality that so few men can ever be the adventurers and explorers they dream of being. He compared his work to that of a grease monkey.

"I look for loose bolts in this company, and I apply oil."

His suit, he explained, was just a CEO's version of bib overalls. Big business, he said, was a messy, technical job in which men competed with each other through memos and committees and struggled to capture and hold a title or a bit of turf which in retrospect was often not worth the pain or sacrifice. The ultimate bit of turf was this room—the boardroom.

He stood before the projector, the image tiny on his broad chest, the bars of the chart zigging and zagging with watery transparency over his lapels and the regimental stripes of his necktie.

"I believe I became President and CEO of this company through my commitment to and relentless pursuit of perfection. I tolerate nothing less. Even a paper clip out of place on my desk first thing in the morning will make my blood boil. I have no patience for sloppiness, passivity, apathy. Not in our management ranks, not in myself."

He went on to describe what they could expect from him, not just over the next year but in the remainder of his career with the company. Then he removed the famous, blue-black snubby revolver from its holster and put the short barrel to his temple, where it looked like a toy.

"If I ever slip up, I personally will take the corrective steps."

He replaced the gun in its holster, and apologized for the theatrics.

"I am not threatening you, gentlemen. I am attempting to make a simple point. My work is my life, nothing comes after it. This is why I don't give a damn about retirement benefits, a pension, or deferred compensation. If you're going to pay me, *pay me now.*"

He thanked them and left the room.

Appleton began the discussion with a few general questions regarding methods and survey participation. He expressed his opinion that the compensation for those executives below CEO presented no serious problems. Salary ranges could be adjusted and participants could be added to or subtracted from the plan at their own discretion. However, he had reservations about their recommendations for Ransome.

The Benefact executives nodded and began to do what they did best: formulate opinions, expostulate, argue. Kimberly, his elbows on the table, his fingers laced, took the position that H&L had exceeded the limitations of the project by proposing a whole new compensation plan when what they had been hired to do was position compensation levels. Pike replied, agreeing that they had indeed taken the project a step further than had been originally planned: BC was getting more than its money's worth. He straightened the stack of transparencies. Blair waved a hand and wanted to know why it was so important to have the compensation linked to the company's performance. It seemed to him that a good appraisal process took more factors into consideration, such as personal characteristics, motivation, commitment, appearance, and so forth. Weren't these just as important as the company's performance, which, as they all knew, was ruled by outside forces such as inflation and interest rates, factors they could not control?

Pike countered that H&L was not proposing BC abandon the appraisal system. The systems should work harmoniously. Goals, however, were critical, particularly for those executives in a position to effect the company's day-to-day performance. Furthermore, it was relative performance which was important: Benefact versus its competition. Interest rates and inflation would affect BC's competition in much the same way it affected BC. With a strategic compensation plan, an incentive existed to deal more effectively than the competition with the adverse economic conditions.

Fowler interrupted. "It is an irrefutable fact that no two companies are the same. So how can you realistically compare BC with the sample group if their lines of business, their size, their strategies, their debt structure are not identical?"

"Of course these companies are different. But they are also your competition and the companies which, together with yours, make up ninety-five percent of the market."

Relative performance was the only fair and realistic means of measuring a company's success, said Pike. "You are in competition. If you agree with that, you have no meaningful alternative. Now, the sample may change depending on what happens in the industry. Every few years the sample selection criteria should be reassessed and reapplied to the companies in the industry."

"It's a nice arrangement for you, isn't it, gentlemen?" Bowles said, his droopy lower lip remaining stationary as he spoke. "Once you've built our swimming pool, you get to service it."

Fowler nodded.

"Now see here, Beauregard," said Appleton, "you and your boys have done a first-rate job, I'm sure, with all this analysis. Shows you just what's happening. But we on the Board think Jack has done a fine job and that the stock shows it. We just want to know if you agree with us that he's got a bonus coming to him. You can let us take care of how to pay him, in stock or cash. Our compensation manager can handle that. We even think we know what we want to pay him."

He burped softly and swallowed. "We need your okay, and you can understand why." He jabbed his finger at Beauregard. "There are stockholders out there who are going to think this bonus is money which should fall right through to the bottom line and be reflected in earnings per share, but EPS isn't what's hurting us here. We've got an obligation to reward the leadership of Jack Ransome, because if he's not justly compensated he'll get up and walk out of here the way he did ten minutes ago. We'll lose him to the first headhunter who comes along. So what do you say, Beauregard? Can we put this handsome report aside for the time being and get down to numbers?"

To Caleb the report represented ten weeks' work—more than that, ten weeks of his life. "Numbers?" he blurted, raising the report, "These are the numbers!"

Beauregard kicked him hard in the shin.

"Thank you, Caleb, for your input," said Appleton, plainly irritated.

Beauregard's face reddened.

Kimberly spoke up, his voice a flute. "I agree with our Chairman. This plan is too theoretical. We want EPS, not ESP."

Appleton continued, "Mr. Beauregard, we have got to deliver the better mousetrap. Unless we do, this company will flounder. Jack Ransome is our best bet."

Fowler seconded the Chairman.

"It sounds to me," Beauregard said, "as though we have had a communications problem, which is regrettable because at Hooker & Lyman we pride ourselves on our sensitivity in matters pertaining to client-handling. Jim Pike will agree with me that we must take responsibility."

What, he asked, did they propose?

Appleton said they would like to pay Ransome another $500,000 in bonus.

How easy it was for the men at the top to get rich. All it took, thought Caleb, was a stock-option plan with generous grants, a discretionary bonus policy loosely managed, or an error in arithmetic—a plus instead of a minus in the funding formula—and suddenly there was money to give away. And given the technical nature of these plans, could a shareholder reading a proxy statement possibly understand them?

Caleb watched Pike, who was brushing specks of eraser from the tabletop. Everything in front of him was tidy and in place. If Pike objected strongly to what he was hearing, he was certain to lose the promotion to partner and even risk losing his job. If Pike didn't object, wasn't that a form of endorsement? Perhaps he would simply ignore Beauregard, pretend he didn't hear.

"At H&L we feel you should not underestimate the nutritive aspects of compensation," said Beauregard.

Pike slumped in his chair.

"Then you support our proposal," said Appleton forcefully.

"Wholeheartedly."

23.

Chapter Eleven

WAITING for the elevator on the fiftieth floor of the Benefact Corp. Building, Beauregard pushed the button a third time. The project team was alone. Caleb's stomach growled hungrily, and he apologized for it. If Ransome hadn't been rich already, thought Caleb, he was now. H&L had just helped to produce a millionaire. As Caleb's father would have said, Ransome's ship had come in: half a million dollars in a single afternoon. Pike stared down at his shoes.

"They appeared pleased," said Beauregard, and he continued without waiting for a response. "You see—and I've said this before—to a guy like Ransome it's not getting rich that's important. It's staying ahead of the field."

Pike remained silent.

"I wonder if Ransome will ever go into politics. Certainly loves to hear himself speak. You all right?"

"I feel cheap," said Pike. "Like a whore."

"That relative-performance stuff may come in handy on another assignment. You just never know."

Pike didn't answer.

"Why don't you both take the afternoon off? Why don't the three of us take the afternoon off? I believe we've earned it."

"Earned what?" asked Pike.

Beauregard stepped closer to Pike. "You don't believe in compromise, do you, my friend?"

"Compromise you call it."

"You should be damned glad it went as well as it did." Pike stepped back. "What about my plan?"

"Don't go soft on me, Jim."

Pike shook his head. Both men stared at the elevator door. Finally Beauregard broke his silence. He asked Pike if he had any idea how he was behaving. Before Pike could answer, the elevator interrupted, opening with a childish tinkling of bells, and Beauregard stepped aboard, turned, and faced them.

"Get in," he said sternly.

Pike didn't move.

"Get in."

"No, sir. I'm going to walk."

"We're on the fiftieth floor and you say you're going to walk?"

"I need to be alone."

"What the hell is going on here? I think I have a right to expect loyalty from my own staff. What is this, mutiny?"

The elevator doors began to close, and Beauregard had to shove his briefcase out to block them. The doors rattled and retreated.

"Caleb, don't tell me you need to be alone, too."

Caleb looked quickly at Pike.

"Caleb, I'm a friend of your father," said Beauregard.

Patronage, nepotism. The message was that Caleb owed everything to the good will of his elders, and that to disobey them was to violate tradition, betray his father, and abandon his career. He wanted to say, "You'll have to drag me aboard that elevator," but that was just a fantasy, a wish like many others. A year ago, graduating from college, he had no idea how much was at stake in the struggle for success—how tough the jobs were to come by and the amount of work they required. He was not about to make a rash decision, a snap judgment, particularly in that gray area between obvious right and wrong. The thing to do was to learn to accommodate other point of views. Once he might have questioned the propriety of compromise, but after learning what things cost, he could see that there was no such thing as an absolute. You had to settle for partial solutions and allow for errors in arithmetic. Firm in the knowledge that he was now a more practical man, that his job was the foundation on which he stood and which made him reliable and respectable, he stepped—irrevocably— aboard.

Caleb felt weightless as the elevator dropped.

242

"He'll come around," said Beauregard.

Caleb shrugged.

"We tried," said Beauregard. "I think we have reason to be pleased with our performance."

The elevator shimmied.

"What's the worst thing that can happen? BC goes under and we get some bad publicity. Well, frankly, in this field even bad publicity is good for business."

Hot, Caleb pulled at his collar.

"An interesting assignment, wouldn't you say, Caleb? You can see why I never get tired of this work." He peered at Caleb to get his reaction. "You'll be able to tell your grandchildren you did business with George Appleton and Jack Ransome."

I'm having trouble breathing, thought Caleb. There's no oxygen in here, and Beauregard is blathering about grandchildren.

They must have passed fifty floors and yet they were still descending. Caleb, feeling dizzy, put his hand against the warm stainless-steel wall and left a print. With his index finger he began to draw a tick-tack-toe board.

"Caleb, I am not unaware of the effort you put into this assignment. I plan to call your father to tell him how pleased we are with you, how well it has all worked out."

Caleb fingerprinted.

"Don't you have anything to say?"

"I could use a drink of water."

"Water? How about a martini!"

They rode the rest of the way in silence. When the elevator came to rest and the doors opened, there was a rush of coolness. Together they crossed the lobby and pushed through the revolving doors. Outside rain was falling in beads. Caleb gulped the moist air.

"Share a cab?" asked Beauregard.

"I forgot my raincoat."

"You mean up there?" Beauregard gave Caleb a concerned look, but after a moment he seemed reassured, even confident, that Caleb could be trusted.

"Let's shake, then," he said.

Caleb allowed Beauregard's hand to squeeze his.

"Treat yourself to a nice dinner on the client. And get a good night's sleep."

A cab pulled up; Beauregard climbed in and, waving, was gone.

Standing on the curb in the rain, Caleb knew he could not go back for the coat. It wasn't just the possibility of encountering Pike: he didn't want to see anyone who had been at the presentation, anyone who might have seen him, afterward, smile and shake hands with the sodden Appleton, anyone who might have overheard his promise to pass on the fraternal best wishes from the Chairman of Benefact Corp to the President of Olympus Brands.

He looked up into the rain and the drops splashed on his forehead. The rain reached down his back with cool fingers and darkened the shoulders of his poplin suit. He licked off his lips the salt-and-soot taste of the city.

On the curb was a phone booth. He stepped into it and searched in his pockets for change. He dialed information and then dialed the Plaza, and after a moment was connected with the Landrys' room.

"Mrs. Landry?"

"Yes?" The voice sounded more puzzled than concerned.

"This is Caleb Sparrow. I'm a colleague of Diane's. How is she?"

"You are at H&L?"

"Yes, ma'am."

"How good a friend are you?"

He could anticipate the next question: "Then why did you let my daughter become a drug addict?"

"Not very, I'm afraid," said Caleb, answering honestly. "I wasn't aware of her problem."

"I see. She is *fair*, Mr. Sparrow. We're relieved to hear her doctor thinks it's a temporary condition."

"Can you give her a message?"

"Of course."

"Tell her Caleb cares. . . . No, let me rephrase that." Caleb tapped the Plexiglas booth with his forefinger. "Tell her I'm sorry. . . . Just tell her I'm worried about her."

"I'll tell her, Mr. Sparrow."

"You can tell her, too, that I'll be in to see her as soon as she is permitted visitors."

"I'm sure she will be happy to hear that."

He could hear the melody of a soap opera. Was Mr. Landry, the lawyer, also there—watching television?

"How does she look, Mrs. Landry?"

"Disgustingly thin."

"Oh. . . . I thought she was always thin."

Caleb rested his forehead against the Plexiglas; the receiver felt heavy in his hand. He spoke softly.

"I'm in love with your daughter, Mrs. Landry."

"Yes, I understand, Mr. Sparrow." She was no longer listening. "And thank you for calling."

A dial tone followed and Caleb hung up the receiver.

He tried to remember at what point in his youth he had packed away his collection of bird books and decided not to pursue ornithology as a vocation, but he could recall no particular day. It was as if the decision had been made for him. Perhaps after he finished Mr. Tapolletti's participant report he could take his vacation and visit the Big Thicket in Eastern Texas—a biological crossroad of Appalachian forest, river-bottom bogs, and flood plains famous for its rich assortment of plants and birds. There he could add to his life list, backpacking through the uplands, past giant cypresses and live oaks clad in Spanish moss and pale green resurrection fern, past orchids, spiderwort, and self-heal, past palmettos, gallberry holly, and sweet bay.

One thousand seven hundred and eighty species representing ninety-seven families of birds were living and breeding on the continent of North America. A bird watcher who had sighted 400 of the 445 Eastern species could consider himself a professional.

Caleb considered himself a professional.

Deep in the Big Thicket he would raise his field glasses at the sound of a hollow drumming overhead and bring into focus the white wing patches and blood-red crest of the male ivory-billed woodpecker, long thought extinct.

The next morning in Beauregard's office, with Pike in attendance, Caleb Sparrow was promoted.

Christopher Knowlton was educated at The Phillips Exeter Academy and Harvard College. He spent two years in New York working in publishing and management consulting before moving to the Berkshires to write fiction. Since then he has taught at Berkshire School and worked as the maitre d' at a local restaurant. As a skier and tennis player he is a journeyman, but he plays a shrewd game of croquet. He is twenty-eight years old, and *The Real World* is his first novel.